CW00969550

R E T :

RETICENCE

Jean-Philippe Toussaint

translated by John Lambert

Dalkey Archive Press

Champaign | Dublin | London

Originally published in French as *La Réticence* by Éditions de Minuit, 1991
Copyright © 1991 by Éditions de Minuit
Translation copyright © 2012 by John Lambert
First edition, 2012
All rights reserved

Library of Congress Cataloging-in-Publication Data

Toussaint, Jean-Philippe.
[Reticence. English]
Reticence / Jean-Philippe Toussaint ; translated by John Lambert. -- 1st ed.
p. cm.
ISBN 978-1-56478-710-1 (pbk. : alk. paper)
I. Lambert, John, 1960- II. Title.
PQ2680.O86A2 2012
843'.914--dc23

2012001861

Partially funded by a grant from the Illinois Arts Council, a state agency

Ouvrage publié avec l'aide du Ministère français chargé de la Culture –
Centre national du livre

This book was published with the support of the French Ministry of Culture –
Centre national du livre

Cet ouvrage, publié dans le cadre du programme d'aide à la publication, bénéficie
du soutien du Ministère des Affaires Etrangères et du Service Culturel de l'Ambassade
de France représenté aux Etats-Unis

This work received support from the French Ministry of Foreign Affairs and the Cultural Services
of the French Embassy in the United States through their publishing assistance program

Cet ouvrage a été publié avec le soutien de la Communauté française

This work was published with the support of the French Community of Belgium

www.dalkeyarchive.com

Printed on permanent/durable acid-free paper and bound in the United States of America
Cover: design and composition by Sarah French; illustration by Nicholas Motte

I

There was a dead cat in the harbor that morning, a black cat floating slowly on the surface of the water alongside a small boat. It was straight and stiff, and a decomposed fish head hung from its mouth out of which protruded a broken strand of fishing line two or three inches in length. At the time I'd simply imagined the fish head was all that remained of a piece of bait. The cat must have leaned out over the water to catch hold of the fish, and once he'd caught it the hook had become snagged in his mouth, he'd lost his balance and fallen in. The water in the port was very dark where I was, but from time to time I could make out a school of fish swimming silently down below, wrasse or mullet, while down at the bottom among the seaweed and stones swarming myriads of fry went at the gutted corpse of a decomposed moray eel. Before moving on I lingered for a moment on the jetty looking at the dead cat, which continued to drift slowly back and forth in the harbor, first to the left then to the right, following the imperceptible flux and reflux of the current on the surface of the water.

I'd arrived at Sasuelo at the end of October. It was autumn already and the tourist season was drawing to a close. A taxi had dropped me off with my bags and suitcases one morning on the village square. The driver helped me unfasten my son's stroller from the roof rack on top of the car, an old 504 Diesel that he'd left running and whose motor continued to purr leisurely on the square. Then he'd pointed me in the direction of the only hotel in the vicinity, which I knew because I'd stayed there once already. I left my bags and suitcases near a bench and headed off toward the hotel with my son, who I'd sat in his stroller in front of me and who was oblivious to everything, absorbed as he was in the contemplation of his stuffed seal. This he examined from all sides, turning it over and over in his hands while burping unflappably from time to time with a royal disposition. A little flower-lined staircase led up to the hotel entrance with a double glass door, and I took the stroller in my arms and mounted the short flight of steps. No sooner had I pushed open the door than I found myself in the presence of the owner, who was squatting on the tiling with a cloth in his hands and now lifted his head suspiciously at the stroller I was still holding in my arms. Not knowing quite where to place it, as the floor seemed so clean and lovingly maintained, I held onto it and asked him if it would be possible to have a room for a couple of nights, three or four nights or perhaps more, until the end of the week, I wasn't quite sure myself.

During my first few days in Sasuelo I spent my time taking long walks, sometimes along the narrow streets that led up to the neighboring villages, sometimes exploring the wild beach that stretched out for a mile or so behind the village. The sound of the wind and the waves blended in my mind as I walked slowly along the shore. It was an immense, deserted beach, continuously swept by swirling winds. I stopped and sat down on the sand from time to time and, while all around me filaments of dried seaweed blew toward the dunes, I absently collected a stone or two and threw them lazily into the sea. My son watched me with a biscuit in his hand, strapped firmly in his stroller by a little harness. Occasionally he leaned forward and tried to grab something or other that had washed up onto the beach, and as time went on I handed him everything he desired, beached pieces of driftwood shaped like strange talismans, pebbles, and twigs (as well as an old plastic sandal, whose sandy sole he kissed while letting out little squeals of joy).

Back at the hotel I spent hours lying on the metal bed in the center of the room. I did nothing and wasn't waiting for anything in particular. The walls around me were humid and dirty, covered with old orange wallpaper that matched the dark flowers on the bedspread and curtains. I'd installed my son's travel cot beside me in the room, a small and rather practical little folding bed fitted together with different-colored metal tubes to form a rectangular frame, a sort of little Centre Georges Pompidou erected beside my bags and suitcases in the dim light of the room. Sometimes, as my son slept peacefully with one little arm folded like a shield across his chest and his treasured plastic sandal placed carefully beside him in the cot, I got up and walked around the room in my socks. I went over to the window and lifted the curtain to look out onto the road, a deserted swath of road running along a weed-covered lot at the back of which, beside a desiccated fig tree bending under the weight of its dead branches, a solitary donkey grazed on fennel sprouts among various bits of refuse, old planks, abandoned tires, and an upturned rowboat that rotted where it lay.

To a certain extent if I'd come to Sasuelo it was to see the Biaggis. Until now, however, held back by a mysterious apprehension, I'd always put off the moment of going to visit them and steered clear of the area around their house when I went for walks in the village. Even on the day of my arrival, when I was still planning on going over to their place as soon as I'd got settled into the hotel, I'd stayed in my room all afternoon. Two days had now gone by since then and I was starting to wonder at the fact that I hadn't yet bumped into them in the village, even if I'd been careful to avoid their house every time I went out. One evening, however, after lingering in the hotel dining room after dinner, I finally decided to drop in on them, very briefly I thought, just to say hello.

The Biaggis' house was situated somewhat outside the village on the road leading up to the next hamlet. It was protected from the outside by a rather high stone wall, which was covered by a tangle of withered ivy that spread out from a thick network of gnarled gray roots and meandered along the rock. A few big trees, pines and palms, were planted here and there in the garden and could be made out through the gate leading into the property. Night had fallen now and the contours of the villa were visible in the shadows behind the bars of the gate. The house had gone up recently, it was long and low, fronted by a tiled terrace where a few pieces of white iron garden furniture had been left outside beside an enigmatic, dilapidated garden umbrella that lay half open on the ground. An old gray Mercedes was parked on the little gravel driveway leading over to the garage, and I noticed that the front fender was dented. I'd never seen the car before, and was just wondering what it was doing there when I heard a sound coming from behind the house, from behind the garage to be exact, like a falling rake immediately followed by hurried steps. I listened attentively but everything was silent around me. There wasn't a sound in the night, and all of the shutters in the Biaggis' villa were closed—as were the metal blinds over the bay window and the pale wooden shutters of the rooms on the first floor.

I stood there on the side of the road looking at the house for another moment, and was just about to go back to the hotel when I noticed a mailbox on the gate, hanging in the darkness at about chest height, fixed loosely to one of the bars with a twisted bit of wire. Even though it looked old and rusty the box was locked, and resisted when I tried to lift the little metal lid. I didn't force it and, slipping my fingers into the crack, I had no difficulty removing the six letters inside. I examined them absently for a moment and saw that they were all very recent—the last one dating from October twenty-fourth—before putting two letters that looked like junk mail back into the box and keeping the others, which I slipped into my pocket. Of course, among the four I'd immediately recognized my own letter, which I'd posted from Paris a couple of days earlier. I could perfectly well have left it in the box, but perhaps there was no reason—no longer in any case—to leave a letter there announcing my presence in Sasuelo.

The next morning at around ten a taxi came to pick me up at the hotel. We'd left the village and had been driving for some time along a rainy road that led uphill among the trees. My son sat beside me in the back, his legs spread on the seat and his two feet clad in little leather boots that stuck straight up in the air. One of his hands was lying on my leg, and with the other he clutched his stuffed seal against his anorak. A transparent plastic nipple in his mouth, he looked at me with a terribly serious, thoughtful air. The driver hadn't said a word since we'd left the hotel. A corn-paper cigarette was wedged between his lips, which he couldn't remove from his mouth moreover because he had to keep both hands on the wheel to negotiate the numerous curves, to the point where not surprisingly his face became slightly flushed and a wisp of smoke played around his ears. For my part I drowsed on the back seat, looking vaguely at the smoke that wafted hesitantly over the driver's temples and formed an immaterial halo about his head, which it soon enshrouded in a splendid evanescent ring. I'd gotten his telephone number that morning and called him shortly before ten o'clock to take me to the little neighboring port of Santagralo, where I wanted to do some shopping.

Santagralo wasn't very busy in the winter but fifty or so pleasure craft were anchored there permanently and, aside from a few shops specializing in marine supplies, there was a post office and a bank, a supermarket and a couple of restaurants. I was planning to stay and have lunch at noon, so when the driver left me on the main square I arranged for him to come and pick me up again thereafter. The sky was still very menacing above the village, and I headed off toward the supermarket with my son ahead of me in his stroller, very upright in his seat and looking intensely in front of him, an immobile little figurehead at the front of our convoy, who deliberately dropped his seal onto the sidewalk from time to time and watched me pick it up with a blend of total indifference and guarded curiosity. You watch it, I said. In the supermarket, as I pushed his stroller between the shelves making a quick note of what I had to buy, he took to thrusting his arm out suddenly to try to get hold of whatever he could, so that I was obliged to maneuver the stroller skillfully back and forth to keep him out of reach of everything he tried to snatch from the shelves. Somewhat put out by my stops and starts, he needed a bit of time to right himself each time I swerved, which didn't stop him from sticking out his arm again as soon as he could and trying to grab something else that was shelved at just his height. Finally, wanting to do my shopping in peace, I asked an elderly woman waiting at the checkout if she wouldn't mind taking care of him for a few seconds, the time it would take for me to go get one or two things. The woman was more than happy to accept and, as I crouched down at my son's feet to explain that he had to stay with the woman for a moment and that he should give her a little kiss on the cheek, my son looked very sad in his stroller all of a sudden. But she's a very nice woman, I said to him. What's your name, Madam? Marie-Ange, said the woman, who'd come nearer and bent down toward my son. She's very nice, Marie-Ange, I said to my son, you don't want to give her a little kiss? Look, like this, I said (and I kissed the woman, who seemed somewhat taken aback, on the cheek).

Leaving the supermarket I walked back to the center of the village and sat down at a café terrace on the main street. There were just a few tables outside, round white plastic tables that had been out in the rain that morning, with a few raindrops still clinging to the seats. I'd lit a cigarette and looked out at the port on the other side of the street, where dozens of sailboats rocked softly in the wind to a continual clinking of booms and stays. Most of the masts were stripped of their sails. Naked and metallic, they rose very high in the sky, with a couple of wisps of cloth fixed here and there to the tops of the spars, little flags or white handkerchiefs, which fluttered in the wind and beat against the yardarms. A large fishing boat was being repaired in front of the port authority a little way off, heaved up onto chocks in the middle of the careenage, and two men stood there talking about the hull by the looks of it, while a third, sitting at the wheel of his car with the door open, watched them talking, intervening from time to time to shoot down any suggestions they made with a sort of resigned fatalism that his companions accepted good-naturedly, as if the man in the car was the skipper and his boat was in fact a lost cause. The rest of the village was very calm, and I drank my aperitif on the terrace while looking over at my son from time to time, who was sitting beside me in his stroller, his eyes fixed on the large horizon. Occasionally a car passed, crossing the village without stopping, and my son watched it with interest, a cookie in his hand, tilting his head forward to watch it drive off without taking his eyes off it for a second.

I'd taken the four letters I'd removed from the Biaggis' mailbox the night before out of my pocket and I looked at them while wondering what on earth could have induced me to take them. Because even if I might have thought for a moment that I'd give them to the Biaggis in person, returning them now struck me as highly difficult without also giving them an explanation. And what explanation could I give? Then should I act as if nothing had happened and go back to their place one evening to put them back in the mailbox? I didn't know. In any case I was thinking it wasn't such a bad thing that the Biaggis hadn't received the letter I'd sent them from Paris a few days before, even though all it contained was a few words saying I was thinking of spending a couple of days in Sasuelo. But if they had received it I'd no longer have the liberty to postpone the moment I went to visit them, and I wasn't at all sure now that I wanted the Biaggis to know I was in Sasuelo. Already on the first day, after remaining undecided all afternoon in my hotel room, I'd realized it was more complicated than I'd thought it was going to be to make up my mind to go see them. To a certain extent of course that was why I'd come to Sasuelo, but ever since I'd felt this initial reticence at going to see them I could very well imagine that my trip to Sasuelo, although initially meant as an occasion to see the Biaggis, would in fact end without my having resolved to contact them—now all the more so, no doubt, since I'd taken the liberty of collecting the letters from their mailbox.

At noon I went for lunch at Chez Georges, one of the few restaurants in the port that stayed open all year round. The walls were hung with old maps in decorative frames and the red and white tablecloths matched the napkins and curtains. Perfecting the punctilious harmony of the decor in a sort of delicious search for elegance in the tiniest of details, the same wooden ringlets served both as napkin and curtain rings. I'd taken my son out of his stroller and sat him beside me on a chair, with his little feet hanging in the void and his chin at table-height. He'd managed to kick off one of his boots and his foot, clad in a light blue sock, imperceptibly beat out the measure of some mysterious tempo. I'd been served my appetizer and my son watched me eat in silence, well behaved if somewhat perplexed on his chair, playing with a few pieces of bread I'd given him to keep him busy. Among the other guests at the restaurant I recognized the man who'd been sitting at the wheel of his car that morning in front of the port authority as soon as he came in. I didn't know if he'd managed to solve his problem but he'd just sat down at a table right in front of me together with three blonde women who must have had the same hairdresser. All three were very becoming and had clearly known each other for a while. Now they smiled and held each other's forearms on the table to a tinkling of bracelets, getting the owner to explain the menu to them, who they also seemed to have known for ages, calling him by his first name. And in fact Georges was also what they called the man from the car, who, sitting impassively on his chair behind his tinted glasses, chimed into the conversation now and then to steadfastly refute every suggestion made to him concerning the choice of entrée. He was dressed in an elegant gray suit and matching vest that compressed his paunch somewhat and, one thumb negligently tucked under the garment to relieve the pressure, he studied the menu while chewing away on a cigar. Oddly enough, as the owner waited beside him for him to make up his mind, he put the menu back down and leaned over mischievously to drum his fingers briefly on the table in the direction of my son. Encouraged by his example and no doubt not wanting to be outdone, the owner and the three women also looked over at our table and started making cooing noises, to which, my mouth full and somewhat caught off guard, I responded with an uneasy smile while wiping my mouth with my napkin, whereas my son, unperturbed by the two Georges, started exerting his charm on the blondes with astonishing cheek, considering his age.

After lunch I went for a walk in the port while waiting for the taxi to come pick me up in Santagralo at around three thirty. I'd sat down on a steel block at the end of the jetty, and I stayed there beside my son's stroller watching a fisherman standing in his boat preparing trolling lines. A purplish octopus lay in a lump at his feet, which he picked up from time to time like an old rag to cut off a snippet with a little knife, holding the blade between his teeth while he bated the hook. Each line had around twenty or so hooks, and each time he cut off a new hunk of bait he dropped the octopus carelessly back onto the deck of the boat with a squishy plop before immediately thrusting the new fragment of flesh onto the barb of one of the free hooks, and in this way he worked his way along with a series of firm and precise gestures. I'd gotten up to go over to the side of the dock and stood across from him watching him work. He'd almost finished now, three of his lines were ready, looking like long garlands of little pink and white octopus bits strung together carefully on the deck of the boat. You're going out fishing now? I asked him. He didn't answer right away, finished baiting one of his hooks. Tomorrow, he finally said without looking at me, and that was the end of our conversation, which had in fact pretty much exhausted the topic: he was going out fishing tomorrow, if I really wanted to know (and fortified with this information I went back to the square to wait for the taxi).

The weather in the village was very gray and a fine rain had started to fall, a regular, unpleasant drizzle that hung in the atmosphere and permeated my clothes with humidity. My son had gone to sleep in his stroller, his little blue anorak tucked snugly around his chest and the plastic bag with the groceries I'd bought that morning hanging disconsolately from one of the handles. The bag was already covered with a thin film of rain, a few droplets trickled here and there down the creased white plastic, while inside it a bottle of water and a few cartons of milk were barely visible and had already started to stretch the fragile surfaces of the bag. All of the stores in the village were now closed, and the square—consisting of a sort of expanse of dirt and gravel shaded no doubt on very sunny days by several trees planted nearby—was deserted. There was a little fountain in the middle of the square into which the rain fell with the faintest of splashes, beside which stood three abandoned, dilapidated benches. They must have been green in their day but they were now almost grayish, all peeled and empty except for the middle one, where a solitary old man was sitting who I hadn't immediately noticed under his cap. I saw the taxi enter the village and drive down the main street from a long way off, and as it pulled up I picked up my son and held him in my arms to open the door while the driver put the stroller in the trunk. My son was still sleeping when the taxi left the village (he was asleep in my arms, I could feel the warmth of his little body against my chest).

The sky over the road was very dark as we left the village. It was just a bit before four in the afternoon but the light was already so gray that it seemed like night had already fallen. The driver had to turn on the headlights as well as the windshield wipers, which rubbed across the glass with a soft squeaking sound. Here and there a fine blanket of fog clung to the wet branches of the trees, and the humidity that reigned on the side of the road even seemed to have spread inside the car, because I was starting to feel pricks of rheumatism in my calves and feet. On the way back the road climbed and climbed under the rain, until about halfway when all of a sudden the view cleared at a bend and Sasuelo appeared down below in the mist, less than three miles as the crow flies, bordered by a uniformly gray sea. The small island across from the village was also visible, whose oblong contours and rocky slopes stood out on the other side of Sasuelo Bay. We still had to go back down the other side of the hill to reach the village, and now you could see the entire route at a glance, snaking its way down toward the sea. The taxi almost came to a standstill at the hairpin curve at the top of the descent into Sasuelo, and we crept past an abandoned church that was practically in ruins before picking up speed on the other side. The road was narrower now, and continued downward in a series of twists and turns between two rows of dense, rain-soaked undergrowth. I looked absently out the window, noticing from time to time the familiar form of some mushroom or other growing beside the embankment amid rotting leaves, a young parasol mushroom or death cap, which disappeared immediately from my line of vision as soon as I'd caught sight of it, leaving no more than a fleeting image in my mind while the taxi had already put over one hundred yards between me and the mushroom that had so intrigued me for a fraction of a second. There was now another car behind us that had also turned on its headlights in the thin mist that clung to the road, and at the last turnoff to Sasuelo I noticed that it turned as well, continuing to follow us from a distance under the rain. I turned around for a moment to look at it through the steamed-up rear window of the taxi and, as we slowed to enter Sasuelo, I saw that it was the old gray Mercedes with a dented fender I'd seen the night before on the Biaggis' property.

The next morning I left the hotel before dawn as the village was still steeped in bluish darkness. A very white pre-morning moon was etched in the sky above the regular lines of telephone wires. All of the houses were still quiet, and when I entered the deserted square I immediately saw that the old gray Mercedes was parked there in the dim light. I approached it without a sound, walking around it to take a quick look inside. The seats were very battered, practically demolished. The leather was completely worn through in places, and there was a three or four inch gash in the middle of the driver's seat revealing a sort of yellowish synthetic foam. A crumpled jacket lay on the back seat amid a clutter of old newspapers and fishing gear, rods and lines, weights, bags of fishhooks, and old plastic bottles. It had rained a lot the night before, and nearby on the ground a large puddle of still water dimly reflected the trees and rooftops of the neighboring houses in the darkness. A light gust of wind occasionally sent a ripple over the surface of the water, blurring the reflections for a moment. Then, slowly, the image recomposed on the surface, trembling for another few seconds before stabilizing, and I saw that the center of the puddle mirrored the silvery shape of the old gray Mercedes, around which, however, by I don't know what play of perspectives or blind spots, there was no trace of me at all.

I walked slowly away from the square leaving the puddle behind me in the darkness, and headed over to the port where several boats rocked imperceptibly in their moorings with a muted lapping sound. I'd sat down on the jetty near a heap of tangled fishing nets still speckled with bits of decomposed fish, and I remained sitting there in the dim light with my coat wrapped tightly around me watching the day break over Sasuelo Bay. The sea was still very dark, with hardly a ripple right out to the horizon, and, as the sun rose behind the mountain, slowly lighting up the far side, which was now topped by a distant halo of light, the boats swaying softly in the port started to take on hints of russet and orange, while the contours of the surrounding docks, fishing nets, rocks, trees, and flowers slowly shook off the bluish imprint of the night.

It was that morning, not long before the sun went up, that I discovered the dead cat in the harbor. At first, from a distance, I'd taken the black form floating between the boats for a plastic bag, or perhaps an old blanket rolled up in a ball, and, intrigued by this object on the surface of the water, I'd gotten up and gone over to the edge of the pier. The body was floating in the feeble light less than ten feet from the jetty, its ears and part of its back just above the waterline. The way it was floating it was impossible to see its face, and it was only when the current caused its body to pivot slightly that I saw it had a fish head in its mouth, from which a broken bit of fishing line protruded a couple of inches. And it was precisely this piece of line that made me think later in the evening—at the time I'd just looked at it without giving it too much thought—that the cat had been murdered.

How else to explain the fragment of fishing line in its mouth? How could such a tough and resistant bit of line be cut by the animal itself? And how, supposing it had indeed managed to cut the line, to explain the presence of a trolling line just a few feet from the side of the pier when it should have been out at sea anywhere from thirty to sixty feet underwater? Why, above all, was the end of the line cut so cleanly, as if with a knife, if it's not because once the cat had been caught in the trap that Biaggi had set the night before—because Biaggi was in the village,

I was now sure of it—he had slowly wound in the line as the cat struggled in the water with the fishhook in its mouth, reeling it up to the dock like a large fish, slackening when he felt too much resistance and quickly winding in each time the cat stopped struggling for a moment, and that, picking it up out of the water while it was still alive and struggling with all its might, he'd cut the line cleanly with a little knife and let the cat fall back into the water with a brutal splash that gradually subsided as the few last wavelets perished against its flanks?

In fact the first idea I'd had that morning when I discovered the dead cat in the port was that the decomposed fish head hanging from its mouth was all that remained of a bit of trolling-line bait that had floated back into the water near the jetty, and that the cat had accidentally fallen in while trying to get hold of it. At first glance, in fact, nothing pointed to it not being an accident, and if several things started troubling me afterward, nothing had struck me outright at the time. I'd never seen the cat before, or perhaps once, although there were probably no witnesses. It had been prowling around the port at nightfall and had run off as soon as I'd tried to approach it. That was the previous evening, when I was alone on the jetty, lying with my head over the water and locked in combat with a crab that had taken refuge in a crevice of the wall. I had a piece of cloth in my hand to protect my fingers from its claws, and in the other I was holding a little knife I'd found not far off on the jetty, and was pressing the flat side of the blade against the crab's shell to try and dislodge it. This had been going on for some time and I would certainly have won out if I hadn't been distracted by the sound of furtive steps beside me causing me to raise my head, the little knife clutched in my right hand. The cat was staring at me intently, barely ten feet away, its luminescent green eyes sparkling in the night.

That evening—I'd been in Sasuelo for four days now and still hadn't made up my mind to go see the Biaggis—I went down to dinner in the hotel dining room after putting my son to bed. The owner served in the evening and his wife stayed in the kitchen, sometimes popping her head in the door to see what was happening in the dining room. There were just three or four guests staying in the hotel, perhaps there were others but I'd hardly seen a soul because my son kept very regular hours. In general I fed him in my room after having set him up on the bed with a bib around his neck, and, as his little eyes avidly took in the contents of the plate, I fed him spoonfuls of nondescript puree from little prepared jars I had reheated in the kitchen. The first time I'd come down with my jars the owner's wife had given me what I have to say was a rather cold welcome (all the more so as I'd brought down a bit of dirty laundry, two or three of my son's footed pajamas), but she'd gotten used to it by now, each day adding something of her own to my son's meal, a freshly thawed filet of fish for example, or a wrinkled old apple that she cut up into harmonious quarters and placed delicately on the side of the plate. My son was now asleep, he'd slept through the night ever since we'd arrived in Sasuelo, and I lingered in the television lounge that evening after dinner. The television had been off for a long time and I was the only one in the room. I smoked a cigarette on the little sofa looking out the window from time to time onto the deserted terrace that stretched out in the night. I still had the four letters I'd taken from the Biaggis' mailbox and I wondered what I should do with them, because I could resolve neither to open them nor to destroy them—at the very most to destroy the one announcing my arrival in Sasuelo. Because I no longer wanted anyone to know that I was there.

All of the lights were off in the hotel when I left the lounge to go back to my room, and I noticed as I walked down the hall on the ground floor that the door to the owners' room was open. The light was on and I stopped for a moment to take a quick look inside. It was a very simple little room, silent and deserted, looking out onto the road. The curtains had been drawn and a pair of stockings hung over the back of a chair. From where I was I could just see that the large oak bed was still made up and a carefully folded negligee lay on the pillow. There was no one in the room, and I assumed the owners must have been getting ready for bed in the little washroom down the hall. I met no one on my way upstairs, and was just about to enter my room when I noticed a little stairway at the end of the hall that had escaped my attention until then. I didn't know if there were any more rooms on the top floor but it seemed to me I could hear a noise coming from above, like the very muffled sound of a typewriter or perhaps a bird outside the hotel, a woodpecker tapping away in the night at the trunk of a tree. I climbed a few steps and peered up to see what was above, an attic perhaps or more rooms, but all of the lights were out and I couldn't hear a thing so I didn't insist and went back to my room.

I'd opened the window wide in my room and stood looking out at the road that wound through the darkness toward the edge of the village. Nothing moved anywhere, and I stayed there at the window slowly breathing in the fresh night air perfumed with the scent of moist herbs. The port wasn't visible from my window but I could hear the lapping of the sea close at hand, whose feeble murmur blended with the silence and gradually eased my senses and my mind. My son was asleep behind me, I could hear his regular breathing from the travel cot. I didn't think about a thing, simply breathing in the fresh air of the night and looking up at the very dark sky stretching out in front of me with several long black clouds sliding slowly across the halo of the moon. Finally I closed the shutters and went to lie down on the bed, where I remained for a long time with my eyes open in the darkness, unable to fall asleep.

When I went down to the port the next morning I noticed that the old gray Mercedes that had been parked on the square was no longer there. I couldn't say exactly how long it had been gone because in my memory it had been parked there all the previous day. I could even remember having seen it when I left the hotel the night before. The sky was still covered that morning, several large and menacing clouds hung darkly over the village. The cat's body was still in the harbor, floating in the gray water ten or so feet from the jetty. It must have bobbed back and forth like that all night in the same small perimeter, bumping limply against the hull of one vessel and drifting between others without ever making its way out to sea. Its prolonged stay in the water didn't seem to have altered its state much, there was still no trace of decomposition or any visible lesions on its body, apart from about an inch-long gash on its right ear—the fur had probably been ripped open by crabs—exposing a small pale surface that looked like it had been emptied of blood. But what really struck me on closer inspection was that the fish head and the fragment of fishing line that had hung from its mouth the night before were now gone—as if someone had come down to the port to remove them during the night.

The following night at around two or three in the morning I left my room without a sound to go down to the port. When I reached the bottom of the stairs, as I knew from previous experience that the front door of the hotel was locked during the night, I started down the hall toward the reception area when suddenly, seeing a crack of light under the owners' door, I stopped and pressed myself against the wall. Had they heard me coming down? Had they only just switched on the light? I stood like that for a moment flattened against the wall, and, still not hearing any noise from behind their door, I started down the hall once again and went into the dining room. There wasn't a sound, the tables had been set for breakfast and the tablecloths shone weakly in the moonlight. On each table, beside the silhouettes of white cups upturned in their saucers, were little wicker baskets filled with small packets of butter and jam. I crossed the room without a sound and headed over to the sliding window. Looking for a moment over the deserted, shadowy terrace, I slid the window open very slowly and slipped outside.

It wasn't the first time I'd left the hotel in this way and, turning around once more to make sure no one had seen me, I left the terrace by climbing over the little chain-link gate that led out onto the road. The moon was almost full in the sky, veiled in part by long wisps of black cloud that slid across its halo like lacerated strips of cloth. The wind blew in swirling gusts causing the treetops to bend and sway, and I crossed the main square diagonally while pulling my coat around me. A telephone booth stood in the darkness, weakly lit by the moon, and a white minivan I'd never seen before was parked a little way off in front of an abandoned house. There wasn't a sound in the village, except for the regular gusts of wind sweeping through the leaves, and I headed toward the port, walking for thirty or so feet along the solid mound of dried seaweed on the edge of the main basin. I could see the port in front of me now, lit by the long beam of light from the lighthouse on Sasuelo Island that appeared fleetingly in the night and swept over the jetty for an instant before disappearing immediately beyond the horizon. I advanced silently along the dock with my hands dug deep in my pockets and looked at the dead cat floating in the darkness a couple of yards from the jetty. The beam from the lighthouse returned intermittently and lit up the cat's body, and each time it came back the animal's horribly contorted face appeared suddenly in the beam, transfixed for a moment under my eyes in a flash of light. I couldn't remember ever having seen the mouth of a cat so wide open, and it intrigued me all the more because if, as I thought, someone had come to the port the night before to pull the fragment of fishing line from its mouth, he would have had to cross over to the animal in a boat and, coming up alongside it under the same moonlight as tonight, exactly the same, with the same black clouds sliding across the sky, he must have leaned over carefully to grab the cat's body—its heavy, wet body that clung slightly to his hands—and pulled on the line protruding from its mouth with a sharp tug, so that now the cat's mouth would have to show further traces of mutilation, it seemed to me, because as it came unstuck the hook must have torn its lips and palate. And just as I was leaning over the water to verify this hypothesis, my passport and the four letters I'd taken from the Biaggis' mailbox a few days earlier all slipped from my coat pocket and fell into the water.

I immediately thrust out my arm to snatch them from the water, but I only managed to get hold of my passport and three letters, the last letter already carried out of reach by the current and swept slowly into the black water of the port. I looked around in all directions for a stick, but all I found was a little fishing net which despite my efforts was too short to reach the letter. Finally I gave up and remained for a long moment on the jetty watching the letter drift over the water, now bumping up against the cat's flank and slowly coming to a standstill, an immobile white envelope floating in the night beside the cat's body, on which a name and address written in black ink were softly illuminated by the moon, Paul Biaggi, Villa des Pins, Sasuelo.

Back at the hotel I climbed over the little chain-link gate and slipped noiselessly across the terrace. I'd been careful to leave the sliding window partway open behind me, and was getting ready to reenter the hotel through the dining room when I saw that someone had closed the window behind me while I was out. I tried to slide it from the outside by pushing with my hands against the glass, but it refused to budge and I was suddenly afraid, wondering for an instant if the person who'd closed the window hadn't known I was outside, or if it was someone from outside the hotel who'd closed it deliberately to stop me from getting back in, someone consequently who was now in the village, who'd been watching me while I was at the port and who was perhaps still watching me that very moment, someone who probably left his house every night and who'd perhaps caught sight of me walking along the jetty one of the previous nights under the same moonlight as tonight, exactly the same, with the same black clouds sliding across the sky, and who, tonight as well, had waited for me to slip outside before closing the sliding window behind me to make sure I couldn't get back in, and who was there right now, just a few yards away, immobile in the night behind the trunk of one of the trees on the terrace. Biaggi, that someone was Biaggi.

There wasn't a sound on the terrace and long shadows stretched across the irregular flagstones, eerie shadows of leaves and branches swaying slowly in the wind. I didn't move and tried to get my bearings in the half-light but I couldn't see a thing, just the very dark, immobile forms of the tree trunks. Slowly I advanced toward the trees, walking straight ahead in the night. My shoes didn't make a sound on the ground, and I descended the few steps that led down to the lower part of the terrace bordered by a little grove of tamaris. The wind rustled through the leaves of the trees all around and I walked on in the night, my eyes fixed on a low rock wall that was being built a little farther down the terrace. A small pile of bricks lay there in the darkness, and various mason's tools had been left beside two large empty cement bags illuminated on the ground by a ray of moonlight. I walked silently up to the little pile of bricks and bent down to take a trowel from an old iron pail. Then, retracing my steps with the trowel in my hand, I crouched down at the foot of the window and, after taking another quick look over the deserted terrace, I tried to unblock the door by squeezing the blade of the trowel into the small opening between the window and the groove. I didn't manage to, and left the terrace without turning around, walking slowly down the road. I didn't know were I was going and walked aimlessly, the collar of my coat raised to protect me from the wind. Finally I passed the battered little sign marking the end of the village, and the road became even darker in front of me, rising up toward the next hamlet along the craggy contours of the cliff. Waves crashed in surges against the savage rocks below, and I continued to walk along the cliff watching the long beam from the lighthouse on Sasuelo Island appear from time to time and sweep over the surface of the water before disappearing over the horizon. I walked on and in a few more minutes I saw the wall of the Biaggis' house appear before me in the night.

I'd stopped in front of the entrance to the property and looked at the villa through the black bars of the gate. The wind seemed to have died down now and the terrace in front of me was deserted. I'd immediately spotted the old gray Mercedes on the little gravel path leading to the garage, and there was no more doubt in my mind that Biaggi was in the village, because the car had been parked there the first time I'd come and I'd also seen it on the village square the morning I discovered the dead cat in the port. Now here it was again, parked beside a tree in the darkness of the driveway, and Biaggi was hiding in all likelihood, how else to explain the fact that I hadn't run into him in the village since I'd arrived? Before moving on I slipped my hand mechanically into the mailbox and discovered that it was empty. I was standing in front of the gate, apparently alone on the road, and was just wondering if someone could have followed me at a distance from the hotel when I saw a set of car lights coming down the road toward the Biaggis' house. I took a quick look around for a place to hide and, pushing on the gate, I noticed that the chain that kept it closed was simply wound around the bars and that a slight push had been enough to open it somewhat. Hurriedly I unwound the chain and entered the property. The car slowed down a bit as it approached the house, and I squatted on the gravel not moving a muscle. I heard the sound of its motor coming nearer, and after a moment two yellow headlights suddenly loomed in front of me in the darkness, lighting up the garden for an instant while the car, a light-colored Volkswagen, drove past the gate without stopping. Blinded by the lights, I didn't manage to see who was inside, and I remained for a moment crouching in the shadows, listening to the sound of the Volkswagen as it drove off, heading—it seemed to me but I couldn't be sure—down toward the port.

It was only then, once silence had returned to the garden, that I remembered that the first time I'd taken the mail from the Biaggis' mailbox I'd left two letters inside, junk mail or bank statements no doubt. Now, however, those two letters were gone. I walked through the garden over to the house and looked at the umbrella lying on the terrace with its pole still inserted in a concrete base. I wondered how the wind could have knocked over such a heavy garden umbrella while nothing else seemed to have moved on the terrace, neither the earthenware jars on either side of the bay window, nor the garden furniture arranged in the darkness a little farther off. There wasn't a sound in the garden, and the grounds around the villa were strewn with dead leaves. Looking up at the façade I noticed that one of the shutters on the second floor wasn't quite closed, and that there was a thin gap between the window and the wall. The hook of the shutter was unclasped and hung against the wall. And Biaggi was hidden there in the shadows, it seemed to me, watching every move I made from the upstairs window.

After remaining undecided on the terrace for quite some time, practically immobile and with my eyes fixed on the shutter, I slowly approached one of the earthenware jars whose silhouette stood out in the shadows. Sticking my hand inside it I felt around for the keys to the garage, remembering that that was where the Biaggis left them when they went away. And in fact I did find them there under a rock, two small metal keys which I took out of a little plastic bag. I'd made up my mind to enter the Biaggis' house, no more afraid of coming face to face with Biaggi than I already was, knowing he could be watching my every move. I approached the garage door and, taking a last glance at the deserted garden stretching out in the darkness, I inserted the smallest key into the keyhole, lifted the garage door very softly, and slipped silently into the house.

The garage walls were hardly visible in the dark, and a small boat lay overturned on the ground. Various objects were stored along the walls, fishing rods and jerry cans containing oil and gas, and two thick wooden oars lay side by side on the floor. Slowly I advanced through a little metal door and down two steps into a very dark, low-ceilinged cellar, where the dim contours of an almost empty wine rack appeared beside a large shelf filled with cleaning products. My eyes were starting to grow accustomed to the darkness, and I left the cellar and moved on toward the kitchen. Everything was silent there, perfectly neat and tidy, there was no trace of dishes beside the sink and a pile of ironed dishtowels lay beside the stove. Silently I progressed through the ground floor of the house. The shutters were closed all around me and from inside the villa they looked very black behind the bare windowpanes. When I arrived at the little entranceway at the front door I hesitated for a moment at the bottom of the stairs. There still wasn't a sound in the house, and just across from me, beside a coatrack on which hung the disquieting forms of an overcoat and two raincoats, was a large wooden mirror whose surface was so dark that although I was less than a couple of yards away I couldn't see the slightest trace of my reflection, just the dense, utter darkness of the deserted entrance.

After hesitating for a moment I went into the living room and, passing in front of the large stone fireplace that loomed in the darkness behind the leather sofa, I crossed the room noiselessly and pushed open the door to Biaggi's study. That was where he normally worked, but I saw right away that his typewriter wasn't on his desk. Some papers and a few small objects lay on the mantelpiece, a stapler, an ashtray, two or three rolls of film, and as I moved further into the room I noticed two letters on the desk. Picking them up I saw it was the two letters I'd left in the mailbox a few days earlier. I couldn't be entirely sure because I hadn't looked at them closely enough the first time I'd had them in my hands, but they were certainly the same kind of letters, two long rectangular envelopes with transparent windows for the name and address, both addressed to Biaggi, Paul Biaggi. And it was then that I thought I heard a sound in the house, an imperceptible creaking coming from upstairs. I listened attentively but couldn't hear a thing, neither upstairs nor anywhere else, just the regular distant hum of the refrigerator in the kitchen. I immediately left the study and went back to the front entrance, flattening myself against the wall. The staircase rose in front of me in the darkness, and I could just make out the corridor at the top of the stairs where Biaggi was standing immobile, perhaps, observing me from the shadows of the hallway on the second floor.

I went over to the stairway and started up. I walked up slowly, with one hand on the rail and both eyes focused straight ahead. When I got to the top I hesitated for a moment, then walked soundlessly down the hallway to the door of the first room, which I slowly opened. There was no one inside, and no one seemed to have slept there for a long time because the mattress was bare, with two large blankets folded on top. Leaving the room I saw that the door to the Biaggis' bedroom was slightly ajar at the far end of the corridor. Had it already been open when I came up the stairs? Had someone just opened it? I was less than four yards from the door and didn't move a muscle. Nothing could be heard from behind the door, and pushing it open silently I saw that the bedroom was perfectly empty in the darkness. The shutters weren't entirely closed and a ray of moonlight entered the room through the small gap between the window and the wall. I walked over to the window, and the room was entirely silent all around me, dimly bathed in a soft glimmer of moonlight that enveloped the walls and reflected dully off the parquet floor. The bed was made and nothing so much as hinted that someone had been there recently, no clothes hung over the chairs, no newspapers lay on the bedside tables. There was no one upstairs, the Biaggis' house was empty it seemed.

But then where was Biaggi that night, I wondered—because I was certain Biaggi was in the village that night—if he wasn't at home? I'd left the house and returned to the hotel following the road along the cliff. The moon was now almost completely veiled in the sky, and standing on the road I looked at the hotel in front of me in the half-light. Its crude white plaster gave the stone a coarse, rough appearance. On the roof, beside the large television antenna that pointed over toward the communications tower on the mountain, the extinguished letters of the neon sign towered up vertically in the night, supported by a crisscrossed matrix of thin metal rods. Four identical shutters lined the façade, and above them two more shutters, square and much smaller, seemed not to belong to rooms but to a sort of alcove nestled under the rooftop. Then I remembered that the night before when I went up to my room after dinner I'd noticed a little stairway at the end of the hall, making me think that perhaps there were more rooms on the top floor, and that I'd been intrigued by a sound coming from upstairs, a monotone, metallic sound echoing strangely in the halls—as if someone were banging away at a typewriter in their room.

Because in fact Biaggi was at the hotel. If he was in Sasuelo that was the only place he could be. He must have taken a room a few days before my arrival with the intention of working there in complete isolation for a spell. Which meant not only did he know I was in Sasuelo, he'd also no doubt been keeping a close eye on me since my arrival, observing all of my comings and goings all the more easily as he himself was staying at the hotel. Because of course Biaggi knew what room I was in, and in fact it was he who'd been hiding from me these past days, only leaving his room when he was sure he wouldn't run into me in the halls, while all the while I'd been certain I was hiding from him and taking the same sort of precautions to avoid going anywhere near his house when I left the hotel. And then it occurred to me that I was probably not the only one to leave the hotel during the night, that Biaggi also left the hotel once night had fallen, and that one of these last nights he must have seen me on the jetty at the port under the same moonlight as tonight, exactly the same, with the same black clouds sliding across the sky, and perhaps he'd even seen me the previous night, because I'd also been outside the night before. But if Biaggi was at the hotel, I said to myself, if Biaggi was at the hotel right now he must certainly have seen me leave tonight, and he was the one perhaps, yes now I was sure it was him, who'd closed the sliding window behind me to stop me from getting back in—and then my thoughts came back to my son in the hotel. The façade was perfectly silent, its plastered walls covered with a grayish efflorescence.

All of the shutters were closed, with the exception of one room on the second floor. Was that my room? Hadn't I closed the shutters before I'd gone out? The wind blew up in gusts and all of a sudden I felt very cold, as if the chill night air had enveloped me in an instant, because I was practically certain I'd closed the shutters before leaving. I was all alone in the night on the edge of the road, and I walked furtively along the façade until I got to the owners' room where I started to rap against the dark and silent little shutter, softly at first, then louder, and, still getting no response, I finally called out. A long silence followed and then, as I was just about to call out once again, the shutter opened slowly and the owner's silhouette appeared in the window, wearing an old undershirt and a wrinkled sweat jacket that hung limply over his chest. I could see his wife as well, lying in bed in her nightgown at the back of the room, and I didn't know what to say. The owner looked at me in silence, one hand on the windowsill. Go around to the front and I'll let you in, he finally said, and he slowly closed the shutter in front of me in the night.

I'd gone to wait for the owner at the top of the low flight of steps leading up to the entrance, and after a moment I saw him trudge down the hall to come open the door. His pajama pants hung down his thighs and his step was slow and cumbersome. He'd left the door of his room open behind him and switched on the yellowish night-light in the hall, which cast a pale shimmer of light onto the walls of the ground floor. He crouched down at the base of the glass door to unlock it and, opening one of the double doors to let me in, he told me that my son had been crying, that he'd heard him crying a little while ago. I looked at him without moving. And now, I asked in a low voice, he's gone back to sleep? He didn't answer right away, and I examined his face in the feeble light. I don't know, he said, I didn't go up, I thought you were with him. I started immediately up the stairs to my room and, as I arrived on the landing of the second floor, I heard a door close in the hotel and the light went out almost simultaneously in the hall. A time switch then kicked in and started reverberating in the darkness, and there was no sound in the hall apart from its regular mechanical buzz.

When I opened the door of my room I immediately saw my son lying in his travel cot in the dim light. The little blanket and sheets were all tangled and he was holding his stuffed seal against his chest. His breathing was slow and peaceful and his hairline was covered in a few tiny beads of sweat. I had an urge to take him in my arms, but I contented myself just to caress his forehead softly, standing beside him for another moment and watching him sleep. He must have had a little nightmare and woken up in the middle of the night, and now he was sleeping with his mouth open, my little guy, his face relaxed and his eyes shut. After covering his chest with his little blanket, I went over and lay down fully dressed on the bed. I stayed like that on my back and didn't move, my eyes open in the darkness. There wasn't a sound in the hotel, and I thought that the port must also be completely silent now, its smooth, quiet waters undulating peacefully in the half-light with the deceptive tranquility of dormant water.

II

It was a little past nine thirty when I left my room the next morning. Apparently all of the guests had already left the hotel because the hallway was perfectly silent when I started up the little stairway leading to the top floor. It was a very narrow staircase that doubled back on itself and led up to a long, dark hallway covered with thread-bare carpeting. Four doors led onto the hallway, the first of which was partway open revealing a sort of walk-in closet where several chairs were stored in the darkness beside an old mattress lying on the ground. The other doors, closed and silent, must have belonged to guest-rooms because there were white plastic numbers glued to all three. So there were rooms on the top floor after all, numbers fourteen, fifteen, and sixteen. Still standing in the hallway I looked at the three closed doors thinking that Biaggi was staying in one of these rooms. Because Biaggi, now I was sure of it, must have come to stay at the hotel a couple of days before my arrival. In fact he'd always needed such isolation to work, and even if I couldn't be sure he'd already taken a room in Sasuelo in the past, I did know he had a habit of working in hotel rooms in other cities for more or less prolonged periods of time. But above all, I thought, where had Biaggi been last night if not at the hotel? Because last night—this I knew for sure—Biaggi hadn't been at home.

I'd gone down for breakfast, and the owner didn't even look in my direction when I came into the dining room. Leftovers still covered the tables, small half-finished packets of jam and butter lay on the plates, and here and there wrinkled napkins were rolled up into balls and abandoned on the tablecloths amid a scattering of crumbs. Four tables had been occupied, which intrigued me because it seemed to me that there hadn't been so many guests on other days. Could it be that someone who didn't normally eat breakfast in the dining room came down today for the first time? Could it be that Biaggi—because I immediately thought of Biaggi—had come down to have breakfast in the dining room this morning? But if it was Biaggi, I thought, why had he come down precisely today for the first time? Why, if he was at the hotel, didn't he have his breakfast brought up to his room as he must have done on the other days? Was he now indifferent to whether or not I knew he was staying at the hotel, or had he realized I'd cottoned on and given up trying to hide altogether?

When the owner brought me my coffee, setting it on the table without a word, he lingered for a moment at the sliding window and looked out at the deserted terrace. It was drizzling, and a transparent plastic tarp had been thrown over the little rock wall that was being built a little farther off, its corners flapping in the wind from time to time. A couple of masons' tools lay nearby in the mud, and water dripped slowly from the branches of the surrounding tamaris. The owner was still standing next to me, looking outside without paying the slightest attention to me. You didn't sleep too well last night, right? he said without turning, as if he were talking to someone on the terrace, and suddenly I felt very uncomfortable. I didn't respond, pouring my coffee instead, and he didn't insist, nodding thoughtfully and clearing the tables onto the tray he'd brought my coffee over with. He moved off, loading the dirty cups onto the tray as he went along. I didn't sleep well either, he finally said, and, clearing the tables all the while, he started telling me about the insomnia he'd been suffering from for some time now, which obliged him to read very late in his room before falling sleep. In fact he never went to sleep before two or three o'clock in the morning, he said, and he slept so lightly that the slightest noise in the hotel woke him up. He looked at me. Was he trying to tell me he knew perfectly well it wasn't the first time I'd left the hotel in the middle of the night?

Because it wasn't the first time I'd left the hotel during the night. Two nights earlier, in fact, I'd left the hotel and gone into the village. A short while before leaving I'd stood for a long time at my window listening to the murmur of the sea close at hand, which had eased my senses and my mind, but when I'd gone to bed I hadn't been able to get to sleep, turning over and over in my mind the reasons for the initial reticence I'd felt on the first day at the thought of going to visit Biaggi. Finally I'd gone out to get a breath of air and clear my head, and I'd walked down to the port and onto the jetty. I was wearing a dark coat, I remember, a gray suit and plain tie, and it was perhaps this very image of me that Biaggi had seen that night as I walked out in the night on the stone wall of the jetty, a silhouette in a dark coat and tie walking slowly in the port under the moonlight which was identical every night, always exactly the same, with the same black clouds sliding across the sky, or perhaps he'd only seen me later, bending down over the cat's body at the side of the dock, as the beam from the lighthouse lit up my face intermittently before plunging it once more into darkness.

After breakfast I went discreetly to the hotel reception, making sure no one saw me in the hall. The room was very dark when I went in. The bluish lights of an aquarium reflected onto the walls and floor, and several fish swam in silence amid miniature rocks and carrageen moss. A banged-up couch stood against one wall and a telephone and a couple of telephone books lay on the old wooden counter in the dull light. I slipped silently behind the counter and took a close look for a moment at the little keyboard hanging on the wall, seeing that while the keys to rooms fourteen and fifteen weren't there, the key to room sixteen was hanging on a nail. I took it from the corkboard and hurried up to the top floor of the hotel.

I was now standing in front of room sixteen, holding the key I'd just taken from the reception, and I didn't make a move, fully persuaded that it was Biaggi's room, that this was the room he'd moved into when he came to stay at the hotel, and that it was here that he'd been working in complete isolation for several days now. He must have gone out, no doubt to take a walk around the village, because I couldn't hear a sound behind the door, and I made up my mind to go in now that he was out. Softly I slid the key into the lock, and pushing open the door I was so convinced I was entering Biaggi's room that I was sure I'd find a dark little nook under the attic with no more than a small wooden table against the wall with Biaggi's typewriter on it, the black plastic cover overturned on the table, an ashtray and several sheets of paper on the desk. There was none of all that, judging from the rayon dressing gown on a hanger beside the washbasin the room was occupied by a woman. The wallpaper was similar in every respect to that in my room, just as dingy and damp, and the same grimy orange-beige color. The bed was unmade and the curtains were open, and a suitcase lay on the floor against the wall. Very elegant, the suitcase contrasted somewhat with the modesty of the room. It was made of soft, padded blue leather and had gold-colored locks, and a tiny key was attached by a wire to the handle. I closed the door and was about to go back downstairs when I heard someone walking along the hall down below, who almost immediately started up the little staircase. I stood there transfixed in the hallway, and the owner appeared in front of me at the top of the stairs, a little out of breath, holding a bucket and broom to clean the rooms. Was it you, I blurted out, who closed the sliding window in the dining room last night while I was out? He seemed not to understand the question, or at least not to make the connection between the window and the fact that I'd been outside the previous night, or maybe he was making other connections in his mind whose consequences I had no way of grasping, and after thinking about it while giving me a strange look, he finally said that yes, in fact he had gotten up in the night because he'd heard some noise in the hotel, and that, when he came into the dining room, he'd seen that a cat had taken advantage of the window's being open to slip inside—a black cat that had run away as soon as he'd entered the room.

So it was the owner who'd closed the window the night before. Unless, I thought, without having really lied to me, he'd avoided telling the entire truth to cover up to a certain extent Biaggi's presence at the hotel, and that last night when he went into the dining room he knew very well that Biaggi was still outside, simply because he'd heard him leave a short while earlier, and that, realizing that the sliding window was open in the dining room, he must have thought that it was Biaggi who'd left it open and so hadn't touched it. And so it was Biaggi who, having preceded me into the hotel on his way back from the port, had closed the sliding window on me, not staying outside on the terrace as I'd thought, but simply coming back into the hotel where he had a room. Because, if Biaggi was staying at the hotel, I thought, if Biaggi had moved into the hotel a couple of days before my arrival with the intention of working there in complete isolation for a spell, he certainly must have asked the owner to tell no one he was there so that he could work in peace and quiet.

Back in my room I went over to the window and looked pensively outside. My son was sleeping behind me, I could hear him breathing regularly in his travel cot, and I went soundlessly over to watch him sleep. He was lying on his back, his little eyes closed and his hands limp, and I watched tenderly as he slept, even somewhat surprised I must say, he slept more than anyone I knew. He woke up a little after eleven o'clock in a soft, almost imperceptible fit of hiccups and tears that grew louder bit by bit, becoming clipped and furious as he tried to straighten up in bed with his head and hands pressed against the finely stitched fabric of the little Centre Georges Pompidou. I took him in my arms and held him high in the air, just the way he liked it to judge from his sudden silence and blissful, toothless smile, before putting him down softly on my bed and getting him dressed to go out, slipping on his big anorak and little shoes. I waited until he was in the stroller before I put on his balaclava (it was always a bit of a bullfight). We didn't run into anyone when I dropped off my key at the front desk, and I picked up his stroller and carried it down the front steps. The stroller was brand new, very light and very practical, and I was really rather proud of it, having bought it just a few days before I left home. It had a chrome-plated metal frame and pale green plastic trimmings, with very solid rubber wheels. The color of the seat was perhaps not as uniform as I'd have liked, because when I bought things for my son I generally looked for the greatest simplicity, preferring simple materials and plain fabric, whereas this was many shades of gray and splashed with a whole nebula of jungle animals, tigers and elephants, even if they were really rather little and quite discreet I must say, blending in pretty well with the rest of the thing. In any event it was very easy to maneuver, even if there was only one handle—the other had broken off the day I arrived and was still in my pocket, together with a wheel clip that had come off two days ago. The road rose slightly and the wheels squeaked (that was new). I stopped for a moment on the shoulder and bent down to see what was wrong, but not finding anything that could explain the squeaking sound I started walking again. Probably wear and tear, who knows. I walked calmly along the side of the road, my son holding his head high as if I'd put him on the lookout at the head of our convoy, a task he carried out with the utmost seriousness, his eye sweeping the terrain under his balaclava—just one eye, because his hood had slipped down and more or less covered the other—watching for anything that moved in front of him, be it nothing more than a dead leaf carried by the wind, whose peregrinations he followed attentively from the asphalt where it had commenced its flight to its final destination on the roadside where it was caught by a clump of wet grass.

A fine sliver of sunlight had found its way between the clouds, and we finally passed the battered little sign indicating we were leaving Sasuelo. Right beside the sign on the side of the road was the municipal dump, consisting of a simple wire container on the side of the road. The cover was open and hung down one side, and the cage was overflowing with cardboard boxes and more or less well tied garbage bags. Some of them, fastened elegantly with little pink ribbons, had been particularly fawned over before being discarded, while others were wide open, sometimes even ripped, whose contents—

open food cans, potato peels, shards of broken glass, fish bones, and chicken carcasses—were spilled all over the ground. The rain had soaked everything, and most of the cardboard boxes were drenched and had burst in places, finally splitting altogether under the weight of the garbage. A foul odor hung in the air and only let up a hundred yards farther on, when the sea air finally regained the upper hand. I continued along the cliff and, as I approached the Biaggis' house—because I was now starting to get close to the Biaggis' house—I started to feel a sort of apprehension at the thought of being surprised so close to their property. However it seemed no one was following us, and the road was now lined on both sides by a dense grove of trees. Soon the wall of the property appeared between the pines, a large wall of irregular stones almost entirely covered by a coat of dried ivy, and I walked alongside it for a couple of yards. The first thing I saw when I stopped in front of the gate was that the old gray Mercedes was gone. It had still been there the night before, however, so someone must have driven off in it this morning, and everything pointed to that person being Biaggi. Because even if Biaggi was staying at the hotel, I thought, even if Biaggi had moved into the hotel a couple of days before I arrived, nothing would stop him from coming and going in the village as he pleased or from using his car from time to time. He could even go home every day if he liked, and stay there for a couple of hours without opening the shutters, sure that no one would suspect he was there. So in fact he could alternate between two separate locations in the village, his home and his room at the hotel, and it occurred to me then that he must certainly have gone from his house to the hotel several times since I'd arrived, meaning that each time he wasn't at the hotel he'd no doubt been at home.

The timid ray of sunlight that had succeeded in piercing through the clouds had disappeared by now and the sky was once more low and heavy over the villa, which was enveloped in a thick gray blanket of mist. All of the shutters were closed and the garden was deserted behind the gate, silent and abandoned. Great quantities of dead leaves were scattered all over the grounds, some yellow and still dry, others ruddy and wet, limp and soaked with water, while still others floated on the puddles in the gravel driveway. This was the first time I'd seen the Biaggis' villa in full daylight since I'd arrived, and it looked very different than how I remembered it from a previous visit, all sunny under a limpid blue sky that had poked through the high branches of the pines and palms. The grass had been dry the last time I was there, mowed short and scorched by the sun, and classical music had wafted from the large, permanently open bay window on the ground floor that led out onto the terrace. Inside the house the depths of the living room had been fresh and welcoming, with the bookshelves barely visible along the walls, while outside a white sun umbrella had shaded the terrace marked by splashes of color from the swimsuits and towels drying on the seatbacks in the sun.

Now the villa was closed and silent, stretching out in the mist behind the wall of the property, and I stood in front of the gate, apparently alone on the road with my son beside me in his stroller. I'd taken out the three letters to Biaggi that I still had in my possession, and looking at them I saw that the brief dunking the night before had done them practically no damage at all. Fine, they looked like they'd gotten a bit wet, the paper was slightly crinkled and puffy in places and the ink had run somewhat on the envelopes, but they were still perfectly presentable, it seemed to me, at least presentable enough to be put back into the Biaggis' mailbox without anyone suspecting they hadn't been there since the mailman had delivered them, and, just as I was about to let them go—because I now wanted to get rid of them as quickly as possible—my hand froze and I sensed that passing shiver of dread I always felt before dropping letters into a mailbox, the second when I read the letter over in my mind, going over all the turns of phrase and mentally checking this or that word, suddenly wondering if I've spelled it correctly, or even questioning what I'd written, and, while my hand still had the option of pulling back, while only a few inches separated the letters from the box and all of these vague sensations blended inside me, it was at this moment that I let them go—my hand completed its movement and I let the three letters drop into the slot.

Back at the hotel I climbed the little chain-link gate that led onto the terrace and walked silently around the building to the sliding window, where I peered into the dining room with my body hidden in an angle of the wall. The lunch service had begun and I could see the owner trudging heavily back and forth between the tables. He couldn't see me where I was standing, and as I watched him I realized I now felt a sort of apprehension as far as he was concerned, a vague fear of being in his presence. As I wasn't particularly hungry I decided not to have lunch, and to take advantage of the owner's being occupied to check out the two rooms on the third floor I hadn't been able to enter that morning. Because I wanted to be sure that, as I thought, Biaggi really did have a room at the hotel.

There was no one at the front desk when I went in, and I hesitated for a moment in the dim bluish light, standing beside my son who'd gone to sleep in his stroller. The door to the dining room was open at the end of the hall and I could hear the sound of muffled voices, a vague murmur of conversation mixed with the occasional clatter of knives and forks. No one had heard me come in, and I slipped soundlessly behind the counter to take the key to my room before cautiously taking hold of the keys to rooms fourteen and fifteen, which were also hanging on the corkboard. I went quickly up to my room to put my son to bed, then left again immediately and took the little stairway up to the top floor. I could no longer hear any noise at all from the ground floor, and the silence grew more and more oppressive the further I climbed up the stairs. When I got up to the third floor I walked a couple of yards down the hall. Before slipping the key into the lock of room fourteen I turned around once more toward the stairway, scrutinizing the curved wall in the feeble light. I knew that someone could appear at the top of the stairs at any moment, even Biaggi, because Biaggi must have been outside at the time. Otherwise I didn't see how Biaggi could have come back to the hotel before me without my seeing him, as I'd been on the road the whole time since I left his property. But now, I said to myself, now, Biaggi could come back to the hotel at any moment and head straight upstairs to his room—all the quicker no doubt when he saw that his key was missing from the reception area.

I turned the key in the lock and opened the door. The room was silent and deserted, and the daylight coming through the window infused the room in a feeble, rainy half-light. The bed was made up against the wall and there were neither clothes nor newspapers; apparently the room was unoccupied. I left and closed the door behind me. There still wasn't the slightest sound in the corridor. I'd now gone over to the door of room fifteen, which was slightly lower and somewhat indented in the wall, and I had a hard time opening it as it resisted when I pushed. It was a tiny room with a sloped roof, permeated by the smell of cold tobacco. There was just one bed and a table against the wall. Apparently the room had been cleaned this morning, but it seemed that someone had come back in the meantime and sat for a moment on the bed, because the bedspread was crumpled and a small transparent, hexagonal ashtray lay on the floor beside it. There was a travel bag near the door, but what struck me the most was the camera and two lenses on the table. One of the lenses was very short, it could have been twenty-eight millimeters, and the other much longer, a very long zoom lens, two hundred millimeters maybe, protected by a cylindrical, padded leather case. Beside it, also made of leather, was a stiff rectangular bag that must also have contained photographic material, films and filters, other lenses perhaps.

Was it me Biaggi was photographing with this equipment, I wondered all of a sudden, was it me? With this long zoom lens with which you can take photographs of someone from far away without being detected? But why would Biaggi have photographed me in the village without my knowing? Or had he photographed me in the port, on the jetty in the port on one of the previous nights? But at night, I thought, even in the moonlight, because the night before the jetty had been bathed in moonlight, always exactly the same, with the same black clouds sliding across the sky, and even with very sensitive film pushed to the maximum, it must be impossible to identify anyone at all in the photo, which would be very dark, showing nothing more than a stormy night sky in the background, the extended, immobile clouds in the moon's halo and a silhouette in a dark coat and tie far off on the shadowy outline of the jetty. I was still standing motionless in the doorway when I heard the almost imperceptible sound of tears coming from down below, the very soft sound of my son's tears drifting up through the ceiling and floorboards.

I went quickly back downstairs where I could now hear the sound of my son's crying more distinctly. I stood in the stairwell, both keys still in my hand, and had no idea what to do. Should I go straight back to my room to take care of my son, or should I first take the keys back to the reception desk? I took a quick look over the banister to assess the situation down below. Everything was perfectly still, and I started down. I hadn't quite made it to the bottom when I once again heard the murmur of conversation coming from the dining room, from time to time a short fit of coughing and a chair scraping against the ground and, just as I was about to enter the reception area, I caught a fleeting glimpse of the owner's silhouette in the hallway. He disappeared almost immediately into the dining room, and I wasted no time in slipping behind the counter and putting the keys back in their place. Then without waiting I went back up to my room to join my son. I opened the door and went straight over to him, knelt at the foot of his bed, and took him in my arms.

I stood at the window holding my son, softly stroking his head to soothe him. He'd put one of his hands on my shoulder and we looked outside as his tears subsided little by little. The weather was bleak, and the road was still glistening slightly from the rain. The lone donkey was seemingly at loose ends in the weed-covered lot across the way, scratching itself nonchalantly against the fence. Look at the donkey down there, I said softly to my son, placing a fingertip on the window and pointing at the animal. My son turned to me and smiled an unexpected and complicitous little smile, still flushed with tears. You see the donkey? I said, but in fact it was my finger he was looking at more than anything else, which he finally clenched softly in his small hand. And that's how we stayed, my son and I, very tenderly for a moment at the window. Then I slowly closed the curtains and put my son back in his cot, because I'd decided to take a nap.

I lay down and remained with my eyes open in the half-light without sleeping. My son had fallen asleep as soon as I'd set him down and now breathed quietly in his cot, I could see his little body curled up on the mattress through the fine stitching of his bed. I couldn't hear anything from outside, and each time I closed my eyes my thoughts came obsessively back to the cat's body in the port, its whiskers like translucent gauze and its ears rising vertically above the waterline, turned sideways and floating heavily on the surface of the gray water, and soon another image—one I'd already seen—appeared to me gradually, the image of Biaggi watching me, and then I saw Biaggi's body floating face up in the port, unmoving, and his arms spread wide, dressed in a sailor's jacket and canvas pants that were slightly pulled up over his calves, his shoes and socks soaked with water. The tie around his neck was ripped and his head was twisted to one side, a bluish cheek slightly immersed in the water. The tie wasn't fastened with a normal knot, but floated loosely around his shoulders like a scarf, and red marks appeared at the base of his neck, faint but unmistakable traces of strangulation, in all likelihood he'd been strangled with this tie. Biaggi had been strangled on one of the previous nights on the jetty with this tie by someone who'd met him there during the night, someone who'd approached him from behind under the moonlight that was identical every night, always exactly the same, with the same black clouds sliding across the sky, and who'd slipped his tie around Biaggi's neck, his own tie which he hadn't taken off and which was still tied around his collar, and which he'd pulled tight while Biaggi's hands gripped his wrists to make him let go, but he hadn't let go, he'd continued to pull in the long luminous beam of the lighthouse on Sasuelo Island that intermittently lit up his face as he tugged harder and harder on his tie, to the point of strangling himself as well to a certain extent, but he hadn't let up and continued to pull with all his might until, almost simultaneously, the tie had broken leaving no more than a ripped clump of fabric around my collar, and Biaggi had relaxed his grip, falling onto the pier with the rest of my tie around his neck—a kick of the foot was all it took to topple his body into the bay.

The village stretched out behind me in the mist, and I walked off slowly in the other direction, heading down to the beach with my son in his stroller, who let himself be pushed along indifferently while swinging his legs idly back and forth. At the beach I took him out of his stroller and he started crawling around on the shore on all fours in his little blue anorak. I sat down on the sand beside his stroller and smoked a cigarette while looking pensively out to sea. The distant contours of Sasuelo

Island could be distinguished off the coast, little more than a rugged stretch of rocky earth. The tiny silhouette of the lighthouse rose up on the left at the summit of the island, and at its very top, somewhat darker, was the little room with the lantern. Large rain clouds blackened the sky and the sound of the waves was close at hand as they crashed against the shore and threw up all sorts of algae onto the beach, plaited like unruly tufts of hair.

As we walked back down the beach on our way to the hotel I left my son's stroller at the side of the water for a moment and advanced cautiously onto a mound of dried seaweed on the shoreline to watch a bird flying off the coast, a cormorant perhaps, slowly wheeling around in circles over the water, and I pointed it out to my son. The bird, I said happily, look at the bird, but he was looking at my finger, a little surprised at having been disturbed for so little, and, coming back over to him without taking my eyes off the bird, I crouched down at the foot of his stroller and started to imitate the cry of the cormorant, kneeling on the sand with one hand on my chest. Cui-cui, I said, and my son at once turned his head toward me in amazement. He looked at me in boundless gratitude, his two little eyes dazzling under the oval opening of his balaclava, and it was as if he'd all at once discovered my true nature after having been mistaken about me for the last eight months. For my part I hadn't had any delusions about my nature for thirty-three years, because I'd just turned thirty-three, yes, the end of adolescence.

Night had started to fall when I got back to the village, and I took a detour down to the port before going back to the hotel. There was no one on the jetty and the wind was blowing hard, ruffling a little piece of red cloth on a boathook that was leaning against the low stone wall. Fishing nets and lobster traps lay on the ground in the dim light and a couple of boats pitched softly along-side the jetty. It was then that I saw that the cat's body and the letter were gone. The water of the port was per-fectly empty in front of me, stretching out silently in the night, and I stared at the dark, untroubled water thinking that to a certain extent we were back at square one, there was no longer a corpse in the port and the letters I'd taken from the Biaggis' mailbox a couple of days earlier were there once again. We're right back at the beginning, give or take one letter, I thought, one letter that had fallen into the water the night before and which the Biaggis would never receive no doubt, because by now the current must have carried it out into the distance.

Night had fallen over the jetty, and I stood there alone beside my son's stroller. Everything seemed strangely simple now, and I continued to watch the black water of the port as it undulated in front of me while thinking that it was even entirely possible that if I hadn't found the Biaggis at home the night before, they must simply have gone out for a reason unknown to me, and that in the same way if I hadn't seen their car at their property this morning, it was because they'd decided to spend the day out of the village and that, having left early, they'd had lunch en route and probably wouldn't be back home until the evening. And it seemed to me then that, paradoxically, as we'd come back to the initial situation in this way and everything was as it had been on the first

day, I could now envisage going to see the Biaggis, perhaps not right away, no, I had to bring my son back to
the hotel and the Biaggis might not be back yet, but a
little later on that evening, just to say hello.

When I got back to the hotel that evening I saw that the television was on in the lounge and a young woman I'd never seen before was sitting there on a couch, flipping idly through an old TV guide that must have been long out of date. She turned and gave me a quick look, and I said hello before picking up my key at reception. Back in my room I undressed my son on my bed and poured him a bath in the washbasin, it was a pretty big washbasin and he was a pretty small guy and he just fit, sitting half immersed in the water like a Roman consul, completely naked with his chubby little nipples, the soap in one hand and my toothbrush glass in the other, with a little yellow plastic duck bobbing against his chest. He played there good-naturedly, every bit the druggist, filling the glass and then emptying it again slowly into the water to see the effect it produced. Generally he was very fond of baths, offering as they did the chance to carry out new pharmaceutical experiments each time, and, even if he didn't have enough room to straighten up and belly-flop into the water, he nevertheless managed to splash with his feet and spill water all over the floor. I picked him up all dripping wet and wrapped him in a large white towel to dry his hair while rubbing his back and little bum, and, lying him on the bed, I wrapped him in a fresh diaper while he beat his legs chaotically just to make things more difficult. You stop it now, I said. He stopped, giving me a charming little smile. He was still lying on his back smiling at me—what a hypocrite—and I sat him up to slip on the clean little pajama I'd gotten out for him. I then combed his hair, parting it on the side (now we're all squeaky clean) and we played like that for a bit on the bed before dinner.

I'd installed my son on my bed with the bib around his neck, and, sitting beside him on the covers, I held a little jar of prepared puree that I'd gone down to fetch in the kitchen, sole in béchamel sauce, judging from the label it couldn't be all that bad, and, while my son looked at the jar with interest, I slowly stirred the puree with a little spoon to cool it down, that's what you get for having it heated up in the first place. A wisp of steam rose from what had probably once been sole and now consisted of a flaccid, lumpy mush covered with a milky broth. I took another bite of the audacious, irreproachably bland mixture and, although it wasn't tasty in the least, it did seem cool enough, just right, I'd say, to give a spoonful to my son who was still waiting patiently on the bed, his mouth open wide to help things along. It's all right? I said, holding out what was already his third or fourth spoonful, because my son had wolfed down his food ever since he was little, so to speak, silent and concentrated, opening his mouth wide even before he'd fully swallowed the previous bite. Once he'd finished all the puree I conscientiously scraped up a last spoonful for him from the bottom of the jar, which I then ate myself before rinsing out the little spoon and jar in the washbasin.

It was a little after eight o'clock when I went down to dinner after putting my son to bed, and there was no one in the dining room when I went in except for the young woman I'd seen a little earlier in the television room, dining alone near the window. She was wearing a suede jacket with a black blouse and little horn-rimmed glasses, and it was only when I went to sit down that I noticed a camera on the table beside her, the same Nikon I'd seen that morning in the last room I'd visited. We were the only two in the dining room, separated by a row of unoccupied tables, and, even if we immediately glanced away each time our looks crossed, I observed her surreptitiously throughout the meal. Finally she was the first one to get up and leave, wishing me goodnight with a slight German accent, and I watched her leave the room with the camera in her hand. It was night outside and I was now alone in the dining room. The leaves of the tamaris swayed very slowly on the deserted terrace outside, and I drank my coffee thinking that the Biaggis must be home by now and that I'd go back out in a little while to pay them a visit.

Back in my room I stood at the window, pulling back the curtain slightly to look outside. I'd left the light off so as not to wake my son, and the only light in the dimness came from the weak bulb over the washbasin that isolated one corner of the room in a yellowish patch of light. There wasn't a sound in the village, and I looked out at the deserted road that led up toward the Biaggis' house. Across from the hotel I could see the lone donkey in the bluish depths of the abandoned lot, lying in the shadows of the enclosure whose rocky surface was lit by the moon. I stood at the window without moving, my body hidden by the curtains that I'd only opened a crack to look outside, and I wondered if someone standing outside might think there was anyone in the room.

The Biaggis must certainly have returned home by now, and as time went on and I stood there at the window putting off the moment when I went to see them, I started to think that if tonight as well it was so difficult for me to take what seemed like such a simple decision as dropping in on some friends to say I was staying in the village, it was basically due to the reticence I'd felt at visiting them on the first day, a reticence that I still hadn't been able to shed in fact, and which, far from having abated with time, had only grown as the days went by, to the point where ever since I'd taken the liberty of removing the letters from their mailbox this had hobbled me entirely and made it all the more difficult for me to go see them. Nevertheless I went and took out a clean shirt from my travel bag and changed silently in the dim light. Then, slowly, I put on a tie and tied it carefully around my neck. There was almost no light in the room, and, after having put on my jacket and coat, I went over to the washbasin and took a quick look in the mirror. I was standing very close to the glass in a dark coat and tie, my face almost pressed up against my reflection. My eyes looked bluish-green and slightly baggy in the dim light, but what I saw above all was the terribly worried look on my face. And yet all I was looking at was my own reflection, which was no doubt not particularly menacing at that, nevertheless the face looking back at me in the feeble light bore a terribly worried expression, as if it was myself I mistrusted, as if in fact I was the one I was afraid of—whereupon I crossed the room and went out.

Everything was silent outside when I left the hotel, and the sign on the roof was still illuminated. The neon lights bathed the road and trees in a faint blue glimmer, and I saw that two cars were parked in front of the hotel. I wondered who they could belong to, and climbed over the little chain-link gate onto the terrace for a moment. There wasn't a sound all around, and I stood in the shadows looking into the dining room where the light was still on. The dinner service was almost over and there was only one couple still sitting at a table, drinking their coffee in front of the sliding window. The man had his back to me, barely a couple of yards away. I couldn't see his face, just the back of his neck and a hint of his profile when he moved his head. Suddenly I reeled back when the owner came into view on the other side of the room. Had he had time to distinguish my silhouette in the night? Had he realized I was just outside the window? I left the terrace immediately and walked off down the road without turning around. I was heading toward the Biaggis' house, and I'd almost arrived at the top of the cliff by now. The wind was blowing heavily, and I continued to walk as the lighthouse beam turned regularly over the surface of the water. I didn't have any idea what I'd say to the Biaggis when I got there, and I knew full well they'd probably be surprised to find me paying them a nighttime visit like that, nevertheless I continued up the road toward their place. Soon the road stopped winding along the cliff and entered a very dense, very dark grove of trees, and after following the wall of the property for ten or so yards I stopped in front of the Biaggis' gate. I couldn't hear a sound from within, everything was perfectly still around the house. Apparently the Biaggis hadn't come home yet because the car was nowhere in sight. I stood on the side of the road and looked at the mailbox hanging in the dusk. When they got back the Biaggis would find the mail I'd returned that morning, I thought, and, going up to the gate, I slipped my hand into the mailbox but felt nothing under my fingers—the letters were gone.

The moon cast a dim light over the park on the Biaggis' property and all of the shutters were closed along the front wall, downstairs and upstairs, and the metal blind over the bay window was rolled down. Could it be that the Biaggis were home nonetheless, asleep in the bedroom upstairs? I unwound the chain from the door and entered the property. Hardly anything had changed around the villa since I'd been there last, dead leaves still lay all over the garden, but I noticed that the old umbrella had been righted and now stood erect in front of the house. Its metal stays were spread skyward, and attached to them were several ripped strips of cloth. I walked noiselessly onto the terrace and along the metal blind of the bay window over to the front door. No lights were visible inside the house, and after taking one last peek through the shutters to see if I could see anything inside, I came back to the front entrance and rang the doorbell. I had rung the doorbell of the Biaggis' house and didn't move, standing there in the dim light waiting for someone to open the door. Could it be no one was at home? I rang a second time, and, still not getting any response, I decided to go in and walked over to the earthenware jar to get the keys to the garage.

I'd gone inside the villa, and made my way slowly through the ground floor trying to get my bearings in the darkness. Anyone home? I called out. Stopping at the living room door I saw the stone fireplace at the other end of the room, barely distinguishable beside the dark shapes of three leather armchairs around a coffee table. There wasn't a sound in the room, and I walked slowly over to Biaggi's study and softly opened the door. I felt around for the light switch and, not finding it, I lit my lighter and saw in the glow of the flame that the letters were lying on the desk. There they were, the three letters I'd returned that morning, lying side by side on Biaggi's desk. So someone was in the house right now, someone who knew I was there?

I left the room immediately and, walking past the large wooden mirror in the entrance, I saw a furtive silhouette pass by in the blackness, dressed in a dark coat and tie.

The night sky was immense and dark, and several long black clouds slid slowly across the halo of the moon. I'd gone upstairs to the Biaggis' bedroom, and as no one was there I'd gone over to the window and opened the shutters. It seemed I was all alone in the house, and I stood there at the window of the Biaggis' bedroom. The garden in front of me was silent, and from time to time the long luminous beam from the lighthouse on Sasuelo Island whisked across the sky behind the treetops. The gates to the property were dimly lit by the moon at the end of the driveway, and I thought that Biaggi—because Biaggi must have known I was in the house—would no doubt not be long in returning, and that any minute now I would see the old gray Mercedes pull up in the night in front of the gate, with its motor running and headlights blazing, lighting up the irregular stones of the wall around the property. I would still be standing at the window of the room and I'd see Biaggi get out to open the gate. I wouldn't move and I'd watch as he got back into the car and, when the old gray Mercedes entered the park, Biaggi would suddenly see my silhouette in a dark coat and tie standing at his bedroom window in front of him in the night.

I'd gone back downstairs and sat down for a moment in the living room without taking off my coat. The windows in front of me were very black, and behind them the lowered metal blind didn't let in the least bit of light. Around me in the darkness I could make out the silent contours of the furniture, the couch and the other armchairs, the bookshelves lining the walls. I sat there alone in the Biaggis' villa and didn't move, pricking up my ears at the slightest sounds from outside, the numerous nocturnal creaking sounds I thought I could hear coming from the garden, when I spied two little points of light shining in the darkness at the other end of the room, one red light and one green light glowing on the bottom shelf of the telephone table. Getting up and walking over to the table, I saw there was an answering machine set up in the villa. I crouched down for a moment in front of it and saw that apparently there were no messages, the tape was still wound back to the beginning. Cautiously I pressed one of the buttons with my finger and heard

Biaggi's voice resound in the utter silence. Biaggi's voice rang out in front of me—Biaggi's voice—vivid, close, and at the same time terribly distant. You have reached eight five three, one three four three. We're not in right now but you can leave a message after the. I'd managed to stop the message and the house was once more engulfed in an absolute silence that was all the more disturbing as I didn't move a muscle.

I'd finally left the house and was walking back to the hotel when I saw a black cat on the side of the road. It was close to the garbage dump, staring at me with its ears pricked, and lying at its feet was a long fish skeleton it had just pulled from a plastic bag. It was no more than five yards away, and I had the feeling it would run off if I made the slightest move in its direction. It didn't flinch and was no doubt waiting for me to leave, staring at me in the night with deep green eyes that were finely speckled with yellow. But what troubled me the most was that it wasn't the first time I'd seen that look, that it was a look I'd already seen, one night on the jetty down at the port. And the hotel owner must have seen the very same look the night before in the hotel dining room, because this must have been the cat he'd told me about that morning, the one that had entered the dining room through the sliding window and prowled around in the darkness, slipping stealthily between the tables, its luminescent green eyes shining in the dim light of the moon, before making off as soon as the owner came in.

I'd gone down to the port and was standing at the end of the jetty, my coat pulled tightly around me. I couldn't hear a single sound in the port, just the murmur of the water close at hand and the sound of the waves breaking against the rocks, and I looked out at Sasuelo Island, far off and barely visible in the darkness. The lighthouse beam swung over the surface of the water, and I watched the long shaft of light thinking I'd never be able to get to sleep if I didn't go to bed now. Already the night before the long, luminous beam of the lighthouse on Sasuelo Island had turned all night in my sleep with a throbbing regularity, sweeping away the darkness and then moving off before reappearing immediately under my eyes without leaving me the least respite. It was always the same dazzling cone of light that suddenly surged forth and grew quickly in the darkness before brutally blinding me for an instant, after which I waited in dread for the next time it came around, soon seeing nothing more than my own panic-stricken face on the edge of sleep, my eyes piercing the blackness, my pupils constantly dilating and contracting with each passage of the beam of light, I lay there staring in front of me, powerless and uneasy, wide-eyed in the night. Because in fact Biaggi was on Sasuelo Island. Dressed in a wet sailor's jacket, Biaggi's stiff, decomposing corpse was on Sasuelo Island at that moment. After floating for a while chest-up in the black water of the port, it must have been fished out and heaved on board a fishing boat that had left the harbor under the same moonlight as tonight, exactly the same, with the same black clouds sliding across the sky. The boat had then putted slowly across to Sasuelo Island, and when it finally arrived at the rugged coastline it had docked gently at a small landing at the edge of the water, and Biaggi's corpse had been unloaded onto the shore under the silvery moonlight, his bloated bluish face violently illuminated by the beam of the lighthouse whose high, silent outline rose up overhead in the night. Then, slowly, the body had been tugged along the little path leading up the rock face to the lighthouse. And there, in the utter darkness, it had been dumped on the ground below the automatic control instruments of the lighthouse that flickered on and off in the night, face up and arms spread wide, where it still lay.

It wasn't yet midnight when I got back to the hotel, and walking down the hall I saw there was still a light on under the owners' door. My son didn't stir when I entered the room. He was sleeping peacefully in his travel cot, and I went slowly over to the window and pulled back the curtain. I stood at the window of my room in my dark coat and tie, looking out onto the road that led off in the night toward the Biaggis' house. I could have telephoned the Biaggis right now if there'd been a phone in my room, I thought. The phone would have rung in the deserted living room of the villa, and after several seconds the answering machine would have switched on and I would have heard the sound of Biaggi's voice in the receiver, Biaggi's flat voice coming from far off in the night. You have reached eight five three, one three four three. We're not in at the moment but you can leave a message after the—and I would have hung up without leaving a message.

It was a little after eight thirty when I went down to the port the next morning. The sky was very gray over the village, and several long black clouds drifted on the horizon over Sasuelo Island. The lighthouse had been out for several hours now, and I looked at its lofty silhouette standing out in the mist, wondering if anyone had been to Sasuelo Island in the last couple of days. Because even if there'd been no keeper on the island since the lighthouse was automated, it only stood to reason that maintenance visits were carried out from time to time and that someone tasked with keeping the lighthouse had to go over to the island on a regular basis. But what I couldn't quite figure out was how often these visits took place. Was it every month, once a week, every two or three days? Because if it was that often, I said to myself, it was certain that someone must have been on the island in the last day or so. And then I started thinking that someone could have seen me leave the hotel on my way to the village that morning, someone who was still in the village and was watching me at this very moment.

I'd sat down on a stone block at the end of the jetty and was looking back at the square that stretched out on the other side of the port. It was empty and the wind blew steadily over the ground, swirling up whirlwinds of dust and old bits of paper. And it was then—as I was sitting all alone on the jetty and there was no one around—that I saw the old gray Mercedes enter the village. It had turned the corner at a very slow speed and was now driving slowly through the square. It seemed almost hesitant, and I thought for a moment that it would continue on its way, but it slowed down some more and stopped beside a bench near the telephone booth. I hadn't made a move and could see an immobile figure in the car, but the distance was too great for me to distinguish who it could be. The car had parked facing the sea about thirty yards away, and the engine continued idling on the square while the silhouette inside seemed to be looking in my direction.

Because it was Biaggi in fact who was watching me from inside the car. Biaggi had seen me leave the hotel this morning when I'd gone into the village and followed me at a distance down to the port. And there he was now, watching me from the wheel of his car, whose engine he'd just switched off. A few seconds went by and a man I'd never seen got out of the car. He was massively built, with broad shoulders and closely cropped gray hair. Was he looking for me, this man who was now slowly walking across the square in my direction? He stopped in front of the little stone parapet at the edge of the gravel and started looking out over the horizon. Neither of us moved, and he couldn't have failed to notice me on the jetty because I was right in his line of sight, with nothing but the softly undulating water of the harbor between us. He stood there across from me on the square with his eyes on the sea, not seeming to pay me the slightest attention. But in fact he had seen me, I knew full well that he'd seen me and that he'd been focused on me ever since he'd gotten out of the car. All the while looking out at the sea, he took a pack of cigarettes from his pocket and lifted it slowly to his mouth, pulling out a cigarette with his lips and lighting it while protecting the lighter with the palm of his hand. His eyes rested on me for a brief instant, as if he just wanted to make sure I was still on the jetty, and then he went into the phone booth.

Who did he want to call? Who did he want to tell that I was there on the jetty? Was it Biaggi, was it Biaggi he was calling? I could see his outline through the window of the telephone booth, picking up the receiver and dialing a number. But if it was Biaggi he was calling, I thought, if he was calling Biaggi to tell him I was on the jetty, no one was going to answer because the answering machine must still be on in the villa. Unless Biaggi had turned off the answering machine, unless Biaggi was at home right now waiting for this call. And it was then that someone answered, it was then that someone must have picked up the phone in the Biaggi's villa because the man suddenly started talking inside the booth. I was still sitting on the stone block at the end of the jetty, and I could just make out the silhouette of the man talking on the phone in the telephone booth. He turned his head in my direction from time to time, and despite the distance I could see his look clearly behind the glass pane, a hard, somewhat empty look that was riveted on the port. Just before the end of the conversation he glanced over at me once more, and he must have seen that I was observing him because he twisted his body slightly in the booth, turning his back on me completely. He said one or two more words and finally hung up, leaving the booth and letting the glass door fall shut behind him. He got back into the car without taking another look in my direction or even looking out at the sea, and I watched the old gray Mercedes turn around on the square and slowly leave the village.

As soon as it disappeared I rushed over to the square, went into the phone booth, and dialed Biaggi's number. Because if the man had just called Biaggi and Biaggi had answered, I said to myself, by immediately calling him back I would no doubt not leave him enough time to switch the answering machine back on, and, hearing the telephone ring again in the living room he would no doubt wrongly think it was the man calling again and he would pick up the phone, Biaggi would answer my call himself. I'd just dialed his number and stood there in the booth with my ear to the receiver waiting for the phone to ring. It rang once, then a second time, slightly shorter, and then I heard the phone connect and Biaggi's voice in the receiver, Biaggi's flat voice recorded on the tape. So in the brief interval between the man's call and mine Biaggi had had enough time to switch the answering machine back on. Because, in fact, he must have gone back out immediately, Biaggi must have left the house immediately after receiving the man's call to come meet me, and he must be on the road right now. No doubt I'd see him appear on the square any minute now. I looked over at the entrance to the village but the road was empty, the two houses towering over the bend in the road were closed and silent. I could see them clearly from where I was in the booth, and nothing moved all around, just the leaves in the trees swaying slowly in the wind. I hadn't hung up yet and Biaggi's voice could still be heard in the receiver, Biaggi's monotonous voice coming from nowhere and talking into the emptiness. Then the voice was still and the higher-pitched, almost piercing beep sounded in the receiver and things were quiet once more. I didn't hang up, but held my breath and didn't say a thing. The magnetic answering machine tape must have been winding in Biaggis' living room, it must have been turning slowly and recording all of the imperceptible variations of my silence. Because I kept perfectly still, I'd contracted the muscles of my hand and didn't make the slightest movement in the booth, while the tape must have continued turning inexorably in the living room of the Biaggis' villa, winding silently inside the machine as it recorded my silence.

When I hung up I realized that there was someone on the jetty. A man dressed in a blue sailor's jacket was at the dock, I could see him in the distance through the window of the phone booth. Otherwise the port was deserted, and I watched as the man walked over to the stone block where I'd been sitting just a few moments ago and passed it without stopping. I was still standing in the phone booth, and I followed him with my eyes while he continued along the jetty without seeming to notice me or even suspect I was watching. He stopped in front of a fishing boat and took a good look at its hull, and after tossing the little knapsack he was carrying on board he jumped in with a single bound, rocking the boat for a few moments before it stabilized bit by bit alongside the dock. He remained standing in the boat while untying the moorings, and, tossing them onto the pier, he grabbed a big wooden oar that he then thrust vertically into the water to push the boat out to the middle of the bay. He was now much closer to where I was and I could almost make out his features, his dry, angular face was chiseled by the wind. I didn't move in the booth and kept watching from a distance, my body half hidden by the gray mass of the telephone. He'd gone back to the stern now and, kneeling down on the bench to start the motor, he gave the cord three long pulls, lifting his arm high in the air. The motor fired up and, sitting down in the stern, he grabbed the rudder and left the port at an extremely slow speed, his body perfectly immobile in the back of the boat and his eyes fixed on the horizon. I kept watching him from behind the window of the phone booth and could only see his back now as the boat headed out into the open sea toward—there was no longer any doubt—Sasuelo Island.

Back in the hotel I'd gone to bed and was trying in vain to get back to sleep. The shutters were closed and there wasn't a hint of daylight in the room. My son was asleep beside me and I lay like that in the darkness, my body covered by the blankets. I didn't want to leave the hotel now, I didn't want to be seen in the village anymore, and, my head full of diverse forebodings, it seemed to me that all of the sounds coming from outside were like so many vague menaces gradually taking shape around me. It was now almost half an hour since I'd left the telephone booth and, lying on the bed in the shadowy light of my room, I thought that Biaggi must be looking for me in the village right now, perhaps even together with the man who'd called him that morning to tell him I was on the jetty, while at the same time the other man, the one who'd sailed off toward Sasuelo Island, must have arrived by now and, having left his boat in a little protected inlet, must have walked up the path along the rock face to the lighthouse where on entering the cabin he'd discovered the stiff, wide-eyed body of the cat lying in front of him on the ground.

I was still lying on my bed in the darkness and I thought that the man wouldn't be long in coming back now, and that as soon as he got back to the port he'd no doubt also start looking for me in the village, and that, not finding me, he'd probably come see if I wasn't at the hotel. I got up and quickly put on my clothes, then I crossed the room silently and opened the shutters. It was still just as gray outside, rainy and bleak, and I looked out at the empty road leading up toward the Biaggis' house. There wasn't a sound in the village, and I stayed there at the window, hidden in a fold of the curtains, keeping my eyes fixed on the hotel entrance whose front steps I could see down below through the corner of the window. My son was now awake, I could hear him babbling away behind me in the room, and I turned around now and then to watch him play in his cot, amusing himself with the old plastic sandal we'd found on the beach a couple of days earlier, trying in vain to fold it in half, his face concentrated and his little lips pursed with effort. Then, still just as concentrated, looking thoughtful and serious in his white pajamas, he started smacking the sandal against the bedpost. And it was then—when I'd stopped watching the hotel entrance for just a moment— that someone knocked on the door of my room.

There was someone behind the door, someone was now standing in the hall behind the door to my room. The door wasn't locked, I knew perfectly well that it wasn't locked because I hadn't taken the time to lock it when I'd come back in, and I stood there in the room watching this immobile door, which wouldn't be long in opening. Another knock came and I didn't move. Then I heard the sound of a key in the lock. Why was the key turning, why was the key turning if the door wasn't locked? Was someone trying to lock me in? Was someone trying to imprison me in the hotel to prevent me from escaping? When the door had been locked from outside—I was locked in now—I saw the knob turn forcefully and heard someone try to open it from outside, but the door resisted. Immediately the key turned in the other direction and the door opened. The owner stood there in front of me in the shadow of the hall, one hand still on the doorknob and a bucket and broom at his feet, and, seeing that I was still in the room, he apologized and closed the door again right away, saying he'd come back a bit later to do the room. After that I stayed in all morning and no one else appeared, all I heard was the muffled sound of footsteps in the hall several times.

In the early afternoon I decided to go over to the Biaggis' house while my son was having his nap. The hotel was completely silent when I left my room and, coming downstairs, I saw a suitcase against the wall near the entrance that must have belonged to a guest who was just arriving or departing. I lingered in the hallway for a moment peering through the glass doors, fearing that someone could be posted there to see if I left the hotel, but apparently there was no one on the road. In the abandoned lot across the way I saw that the lone donkey had come up to the fence and was staring over at the hotel. All of a sudden it gave its head and mane a violent shake, after which it came slowly back to its initial position, gently nodding its head. I watched it for a few more moments, then left the hotel and started up the road toward the Biaggis' house. I'd almost left the village and was now at the bend in the road beside the dump. The wire cage was now empty, and the only things on the ground were several scraps of garbage that must have fallen from the bags when the dump truck passed, lying there beside an upturned coffee filter whose contents were spread out in the grass nearby. I continued along the cliff and looked out at the sea stretching off into the distance, strangely calm around Sasuelo Island. The sky was completely dark now on the horizon, overcast by large rain clouds that the wind was slowly pushing toward the coast. The road had entered a dense grove of trees and was still deserted in front of me, and I'd just started along the wall of the Biaggis' property when I saw that the gates were open.

I slowed down a little, stopping a little away from the entrance when I saw a man in the garden—massively built, with broad shoulders and closely cropped gray hair, the man who'd been in the telephone booth that morning. He hadn't seen me, and was busy raking the dead leaves in the garden. There was a little pile of dead leaves beside him on the lawn, and I noticed that the old gray Mercedes was parked on the gravel driveway a little farther off. The shutters were still closed along the front of the house but the garage door was now open, and in the distance I could just make out the contours of an upturned fishing boat and several jerry cans containing oil and gas against the far wall. The man still hadn't seen me, and continued to rake the lawn without suspecting I was observing him. I stood there at the entrance to the property, my body hidden in an angle of the gate, watching the man move back and forth in the park with the rake in his hand, and, following him with my eyes, I couldn't help wondering if this man who seemed so at home in the garden wasn't simply the caretaker. Everything seemed to point to it, in fact, and yet for all I could remember the Biaggis' caretaker, the man who took care of the garden and guarded the house in their absence, wasn't this man in front of me but a very friendly old guy who I'd seen once or twice when he came to water the garden in the summer and who everyone had always called Rafa, without my ever knowing if that was his first name or his last name, Mr. Rafa.

I'd taken a couple of steps forward and the man had seen me by now. He stopped raking when I entered the property and watched me come over to him without moving. When I got to where he was it was clear he was waiting for me to say something. I nodded hello and he nodded back, and I explained I was a friend of the Biaggis'. He went back to raking with another nod, as if this simple sentence had satisfied his curiosity as far as I was concerned and allowed him to resume his work in peace. We exchanged another couple of words and, as I remained standing beside him on the gravel driveway looking up at the closed shutters of the Biaggis' house, I felt that my presence in the garden didn't bother him at all. We didn't really converse, I just stood there next to him and watched him rake, from time to time lifting a stray leaf with the tip of my shoe, putting it mechanically back in the little pile on the grass, and, as he continued to rake a little further down the lawn, he finally said that this wasn't the first time he'd seen me, that he'd already seen me walking in the village with my son, and wondered who I might be. You're the one with the baby, right? he asked. I said that yes, I was the one with the baby. Yeah, I've seen you around, he said, and I noticed then that he had a little stain on his pant leg, a little grease stain that was quite recent and that hadn't had the time to dry, which made me think—I don't know why—that it could be boat motor oil. The sky was increasingly menacing over the property and soon the first drops of rain started to fall in the garden, very large droplets that were still spaced far apart, suggesting that a major cloudburst was on its way. Gusts of wind blew the clouds across the sky, shaking the leaves in the trees, and in less than a minute the rain came pounding down, suddenly and brutally, and started to flood all of the paths in the garden as we rushed off the lawn and ran to take shelter in the garage, bending down under the pouring rain.

We stood side by side in the garage doorway, our shoulders and faces slightly wet, watching the rain fall in the garden without saying a word. The grounds across from us were very dark and the gate at the end of the gravel driveway was still open. Far off we could see the rain falling onto the road where it formed into two rivulets and flowed slowly over the asphalt onto the shoulder. The lawns were soon completely soaked, and as the earth must already have been saturated with water from all the showers in recent days, in just a few minutes a large puddle had formed across from us on the driveway into which the rain clattered down, splashing water all around. The man stood beside me without moving and finally took a pack of cigarettes from his pocket, and, without a word, held it up to offer me a cigarette. Then, with the same gesture I'd already seen him use that morning, he slowly brought the pack to his mouth to pull out a cigarette with his lips. He searched for a lighter in his pocket and gave me a light before lighting his cigarette. This could go on for a while, he said, taking a long drag, this could go on for a while. He moved off toward the back of the garage and, passing the upturned fishing boat, he went and hunched over beside a big wooden box, no doubt a toolbox, from which he took out two pairs of pliers and a screwdriver, putting them on the ground beside him. I'll be back, he said picking up the tools, and, opening the little metal door at the back of the garage, he disappeared inside the house.

I stayed alone in the garage and looked for a moment at the little metal door that he'd just closed behind him. The garage was very dark, and the upturned fishing boat took up almost all the room. Diverse objects lay here and there in the dim light, two or three spades in a pail, some tools, a couple of flower pots lining the walls. The downpour hadn't let up and the rain continued to fall onto the roof of the garage, reverberating on the corrugated metal above my head. The gravel driveway looked almost like a swamp by now, with dead leaves drifting in puddles all around, while a curtain of rain continued to beat down on the lawns. Ten or so minutes had already gone by since the man had disappeared and I could now hear sounds in the house, indefinable sounds of steps and

118

objects being moved, then the steps came closer and the man reappeared in the garage to say that I might as well wait out the rainstorm inside the house. I joined him in the back of the garage and he led me through into the cellar, shutting the door behind me. But wasn't it a mistake to follow him? Because Biaggi was in the house perhaps. Biaggi was in the living room of the house right now.

There was almost no light in the cellar, a single naked bulb hung from the ceiling, and I followed the man into the kitchen where some old sheets of newspaper were spread out to protect the floor. The door under the sink was open, revealing an iron bucket full of dirty, stagnant water under a bent water pipe. The man collected the tools and tidied up the newspaper, which he rolled into a ball and threw into the garbage before turning off the kitchen light and heading into the living room. I followed him down the hall, where all of the lights were off and all of the shutters closed. When we got to the living room he walked over to the bay window in the darkness and pulled several times on the cord to raise the metal blind, slowly letting the gray light of day into the room. Even when the blind was completely open the living room was still very dark. We could have switched on the light but neither of us bothered to do it. I'd gone over to the fireplace and was now standing behind the couch beside the little sideboard containing the aperitif bottles. Our wet shoes had left traces on the floor, two long streaks whose separate itineraries you could follow across the room, one heading to the fireplace and the other straight over to the window where the man was still standing pensively, a pair of muddy old tennis shoes on his feet, watching the rain fall in the garden without paying me any further attention. I took a few random steps, my hands in the pockets of my coat, lingering for a moment in front of the bookshelf. Then, while the man continued to stand at the window with his back to me, I walked silently over to the telephone and bent down discreetly over the little transparent window of the answering machine to look at the tape inside. It had turned since the last time I'd seen it, there'd been one call without question, no more, a single call, the call I'd made that morning in all likelihood, but no one had listened to my message.

I'd sat down in one of the leather armchairs facing the couch to wait out the downpour, and I remained sitting there in my coat, with my legs crossed and my hands in my pockets. The man hadn't moved from the window, he'd lit a cigarette and was smoking it while looking outside, only leaving his place to come flick his ash in the little hexagonal ashtray that lay across from me on the coffee table. He bent down for a moment right in front of me, his jacket almost brushing against my face, before immediately taking up his post again at the window. A very soft light still pervaded the living room while the muffled sound of the rain continued to reach us from outside, lessened somewhat by the thick windows. I picked up an old magazine that was lying on the coffee table and flipped through it absently with one hand, looking just at the photos or an occasional headline. Finally I put it back down and, setting it on the table just as the man was coming over once again to stub out his cigarette, I asked him why Rafa wasn't there. He took the time to put out his cigarette in the ashtray and, lifting his eyes for a moment, he told me while returning to the window that Rafa had gone to hospital for heart surgery. A vasectomy, he said, indicating the location of his heart on his shirt, where he started to trace precise little drawings with his finger to give me a quick overview of the operation. It's not very serious, he said, but he's got to rest, you understand. I said that yes, I understood.

I'd gone over to join him, and now we were both standing at the bay window looking out. It was still raining outside and the window was dotted with a network of raindrops, some of which trickled slowly down the pane. A bit of condensation had formed, a slight veil of vapor behind which the garden furniture was visible on the terrace. The old gray Mercedes was parked a little farther off down the driveway, the doors and windshield dripping with rain, and I looked at it pensively from behind the window. The man didn't move beside me, he was also looking outside, and it struck me then that the old gray Mercedes must have been his, that in fact it was his car, and that each time I'd seen it in the village he was the one who'd been driving it, and that each time I'd seen it parked somewhere he was the one who'd parked it. And that he was also the one who collected the mail from the Biaggis' mailbox and put it inside the house. I glanced at him out of the corner of my eye. Could it really be him? Could it be, to sum it all up, that the Biaggis had been absent from Sasuelo ever since I'd arrived, and that every time I thought I'd detected a sign of their presence, it was in fact this man's presence I'd sensed?

After dinner that evening I went out on the terrace for a breath of air. There were still a few guests in the dining room when I got up from the table, and I walked over to the window, sliding it back softly and leaving the hotel. The sky was completely clear over the treetops, a limpid and transparent blue-black, cloudless and washed by the rain. A long, untroubled puddle of water stretched out on the ground, and I advanced over the terrace, leaving the low rock wall that was being built behind me on my right. I walked on until I got to the edge of the terrace, from where the jetty and the sea were visible behind the grove of tamaris. The water was calm and silent, with the stillest of waves lapping up against the crevices in the rocks, while silvery wrinkles of moonlight reflected off its surface in the distance. I leaned for a moment against the low wall at the edge of the terrace and looked out at the water, no longer thinking about a thing. It was then that a small light bobbing imperceptibly in the port caught my eye. It looked like a lantern, the quivering ray of a lantern lighting up a silhouette in a boat. I looked more closely and thought I could see who it was, not that I recognized his features at all, it was more the cut of his figure and his massive back and shoulders now covered by a thick jacket.

Down at the jetty I had no problem recognizing the man, and I walked along the pier to where the boat was anchored. He lifted his head when I arrived and didn't really say hello, more like just acknowledged my presence. Not that he was at all put out, my arrival didn't seem to bother him in the least. He was sitting on an overturned wooden box on the floor of the boat, preparing trolling lines in the light of a little metal lantern hanging from the side of the tiny cabin. The hull swayed slowly beside the dock, and the shadows inside the boat shifted as the lantern swung back and forth. I'd sat down on the jetty beside a heap of fishing nets left lying there in the dark, and continued to watch the man prepare his trolling lines in front of me in the boat. You're going out fishing now? I asked him. Tomorrow, he said, and he slipped a fresh piece of bait onto one of his hooks. I took a look at the bait for a moment, a fish head fixed in the darkness to a bit of line. The weather's going to be good, he went on, but I was hardly listening, I was staring at the bait as he explained that he hadn't been able to go fishing all week because of the bad weather. The last time he'd been fishing, he said, was, was—he stopped to think. It was the day the cat was murdered. He couldn't remember, Tuesday or Wednesday, and I looked at his face in the shadows, his massive features and thick crew cut lit from the side by the trembling light. There was no sound around us, just the continual squeak of moorings in the port and sometimes the very short thud of a hull against the wharf, and I continued to look at the man facing me in the shadowy light when I heard the sound of furtive steps coming from the mound of dried seaweed that stretched out on the other side of the port. Hardly had I noticed where the steps were coming from than a black cat appeared in front of me on the jetty and stared at me with luminescent green eyes. The man gave a loud shout that made me start, and hurled the cloth he was holding in its direction, so that it landed with a feeble plop on the jetty.

He then explained it to me in detail how the cat had died accidentally a couple of days ago. Just like tonight, the day before the cat died the man had prepared trolling lines to go out fishing the next day, leaving them overnight in the boat. It was still dark when he came down to the port the next morning, and two black cats had followed him onto the jetty. Just as he was about to board the boat they'd jumped in and pounced on the bait, running off immediately when the man got in and shooed them away. But one of them had gotten a hook snagged in its mouth and was caught by the fishing lines. Struggling furiously, it had become tangled in all the lines on the deck of the boat so that, seeing as it was impossible to get it under control, the man had grabbed a little knife and cut the line to free the cat, which, thrashing around in panic with the hook in its mouth, had finally jumped overboard and drowned in no time as the man looked on. He had then gone out fishing, and it was only later that I myself came down to the jetty, discovering the dead cat in the port and the man's old gray Mercedes parked on the village square in the dim morning light.

I didn't go back to the hotel right away that night, instead I walked down to the big sandy beach that stretched out for a mile or so behind the village. Leaving the village behind me I walked down the little path to the beach, avoiding here and there the large puddles of water that had formed in the ruts and were dimly lit by the moon. There was a field in the darkness on the edge of the path, a silent, abandoned field enclosed by a rickety old fence. Walking along the deserted path I soon started to hear the sound of the sea in the distance, the regular murmur of the sea that little by little eased my senses and my mind. Down at the beach I took off my shoes and socks and walked slowly toward the shore, my feet bare and my shoes in my hand. I felt the cold contact of the humid sand under my feet and between my toes, and with each step I dug my feet deeper to immerse myself more and more in the sensation of well-being that I felt with the contact of the wet sand. Finally I sat down at water's edge and didn't move, looking out at the sea in front of me. The lighthouse on Sasuelo Island turned regularly in the night and everything was perfectly still. I sat there all alone on the beach in a dark coat, my bare feet in the wet sand. A boat appeared on the horizon, a ferry that slipped slowly across the sea all lit up in the night, moving imperceptibly over the surface of the water until it finally disappeared behind Sasuelo Island.

JEAN-PHILIPPE TOUSSAINT is the author of nine novels, and the winner of numerous literary prizes, including the Prix Décembre for *The Truth about Marie*. His writing has been compared to the works of Samuel Beckett, and the films of Jacques Tati and Jim Jarmusch.

A native of Vancouver, JOHN LAMBERT studied philosophy in Paris before moving to Berlin, where he lives with his wife and two children. He has also translated Jean-Philippe Toussaint's *Monsieur* and *Self-Portrait Abroad*.

SELECTED DALKEY ARCHIVE TITLES

FORD MADOX FORD,
  The March of Literature.
JON FOSSE, *Aliss at the Fire.*
  Melancholy.
MAX FRISCH, *I'm Not Stiller.*
  Man in the Holocene.
CARLOS FUENTES, *Christopher Unborn.*
  Distant Relations.
  Terra Nostra.
  Vlad.
  Where the Air Is Clear.
TAKEHIKO FUKUNAGA, *Flowers of Grass.*
WILLIAM GADDIS, *J R.*
  The Recognitions.
JANICE GALLOWAY, *Foreign Parts.*
  The Trick Is to Keep Breathing.
WILLIAM H. GASS, *Cartesian Sonata*
  and Other Novellas.
  Finding a Form.
  A Temple of Texts.
  The Tunnel.
  Willie Masters' Lonesome Wife.
GÉRARD GAVARRY, *Hoppla! 1 2 3.*
  Making a Novel.
ETIENNE GILSON,
  The Arts of the Beautiful.
  Forms and Substances in the Arts.
C. S. GISCOMBE, *Giscome Road.*
  Here.
  Prairie Style.
DOUGLAS GLOVER, *Bad News of the Heart.*
  The Enamoured Knight.
WITOLD GOMBROWICZ,
  A Kind of Testament.
PAULO EMÍLIO SALES GOMES, *P's Three*
  Women.
KAREN ELIZABETH GORDON, *The Red Shoes.*
GEORGI GOSPODINOV, *Natural Novel.*
JUAN GOYTISOLO, *Count Julian.*
  Exiled from Almost Everywhere.
  Juan the Landless.
  Makbara.
  Marks of Identity.
PATRICK GRAINVILLE, *The Cave of Heaven.*
HENRY GREEN, *Back.*
  Blindness.
  Concluding.
  Doting.
  Nothing.
JACK GREEN, *Fire the Bastards!*
JIŘÍ GRUŠA, *The Questionnaire.*
GABRIEL GUDDING,
  Rhode Island Notebook.
MELA HARTWIG, *Am I a Redundant*
  Human Being?
JOHN HAWKES, *The Passion Artist.*
  Whistlejacket.
ELIZABETH HEIGHWAY, ED., *Best of*
  Contemporary Fiction from Georgia.
ALEKSANDAR HEMON, ED.,
  Best European Fiction.
AIDAN HIGGINS, *Balcony of Europe.*
  A Bestiary.
  Blind Man's Bluff
  Bornholm Night-Ferry.
  Darkling Plain: Texts for the Air.
  Flotsam and Jetsam.
  Langrishe, Go Down.
  Scenes from a Receding Past.
  Windy Arbours.
KEIZO HINO, *Isle of Dreams.*
KAZUSHI HOSAKA, *Plainsong.*

ALDOUS HUXLEY, *Antic Hay.*
  Crome Yellow.
  Point Counter Point.
  Those Barren Leaves.
  Time Must Have a Stop.
NAOYUKI II, *The Shadow of a Blue Cat.*
MIKHAIL IOSSEL AND JEFF PARKER, EDS.,
  Amerika: Russian Writers View the
  United States.
DRAGO JANČAR, *The Galley Slave.*
GERT JONKE, *The Distant Sound.*
  Geometric Regional Novel.
  Homage to Czerny.
  The System of Vienna.
JACQUES JOUET, *Mountain R.*
  Savage.
  Upstaged.
CHARLES JULIET, *Conversations with*
  Samuel Beckett and Bram van
  Velde.
MIEKO KANAI, *The Word Book.*
YORAM KANIUK, *Life on Sandpaper.*
HUGH KENNER, *The Counterfeiters.*
  Flaubert, Joyce and Beckett:
  The Stoic Comedians.
  Joyce's Voices.
DANILO KIŠ, *The Attic.*
  Garden, Ashes.
  The Lute and the Scars
  Psalm 44.
  A Tomb for Boris Davidovich.
ANITA KONKKA, *A Fool's Paradise.*
GEORGE KONRÁD, *The City Builder.*
TADEUSZ KONWICKI, *A Minor Apocalypse.*
  The Polish Complex.
MENIS KOUMANDAREAS, *Koula.*
ELAINE KRAF, *The Princess of 72nd Street.*
JIM KRUSOE, *Iceland.*
AYŞE KULIN, *Farewell: A Mansion in*
  Occupied Istanbul.
EWA KURYLUK, *Century 21.*
EMILIO LASCANO TEGUI, *On Elegance*
  While Sleeping.
ERIC LAURRENT, *Do Not Touch.*
HERVÉ LE TELLIER, *The Sextine Chapel.*
  A Thousand Pearls (for a Thousand
  Pennies)
VIOLETTE LEDUC, *La Bâtarde.*
EDOUARD LEVÉ, *Autoportrait.*
  Suicide.
MARIO LEVI, *Istanbul Was a Fairy Tale.*
SUZANNE JILL LEVINE, *The Subversive*
  Scribe: Translating Latin
  American Fiction.
DEBORAH LEVY, *Billy and Girl.*
  Pillow Talk in Europe and Other
  Places.
JOSÉ LEZAMA LIMA, *Paradiso.*
ROSA LIKSOM, *Dark Paradise.*
OSMAN LINS, *Avalovara.*
  The Queen of the Prisons of Greece.
ALF MAC LOCHLAINN,
  The Corpus in the Library.
  Out of Focus.
RON LOEWINSOHN, *Magnetic Field(s).*
MINA LOY, *Stories and Essays of Mina Loy.*
BRIAN LYNCH, *The Winner of Sorrow.*
D. KEITH MANO, *Take Five.*
MICHELINE AHARONIAN MARCOM,
  The Mirror in the Well.
BEN MARCUS,
  The Age of Wire and String.

SELECTED DALKEY ARCHIVE TITLES

WALLACE MARKFIELD,
  Teitlebaum's Window.
  To an Early Grave.
DAVID MARKSON, *Reader's Block.*
  Springer's Progress.
  Wittgenstein's Mistress.
CAROLE MASO, *AVA.*
LADISLAV MATEJKA AND KRYSTYNA
  POMORSKA, EDS.,
  Readings in Russian Poetics:
    Formalist and Structuralist Views.
HARRY MATHEWS,
  The Case of the Persevering Maltese:
    Collected Essays.
  Cigarettes.
  The Conversions.
  The Human Country: New and
    Collected Stories.
  The Journalist.
  My Life in CIA.
  Singular Pleasures.
  The Sinking of the Odradek
    Stadium.
  Tlooth.
  20 Lines a Day.
JOSEPH MCELROY,
  Night Soul and Other Stories.
THOMAS MCGONIGLE,
  Going to Patchogue.
ROBERT L. MCLAUGHLIN, ED., *Innovations:*
    An Anthology of Modern &
    Contemporary Fiction.
ABDELWAHAB MEDDEB, *Talismano.*
GERHARD MEIER, *Isle of the Dead.*
HERMAN MELVILLE, *The Confidence-Man.*
AMANDA MICHALOPOULOU, *I'd Like.*
STEVEN MILLHAUSER, *The Barnum Museum.*
  In the Penny Arcade.
RALPH J. MILLS, JR., *Essays on Poetry.*
MOMUS, *The Book of Jokes.*
CHRISTINE MONTALBETTI, *The Origin of Man.*
  Western.
OLIVE MOORE, *Spleen.*
NICHOLAS MOSLEY, *Accident.*
  Assassins.
  Catastrophe Practice.
  Children of Darkness and Light.
  Experience and Religion.
  A Garden of Trees.
  God's Hazard.
  The Hesperides Tree.
  Hopeful Monsters.
  Imago Bird.
  Impossible Object.
  Inventing God.
  Judith.
  Look at the Dark.
  Natalie Natalia.
  Paradoxes of Peace.
  Serpent.
  Time at War.
  The Uses of Slime Mould:
    Essays of Four Decades.
WARREN MOTTE,
  Fables of the Novel: French Fiction
    since 1990.
  Fiction Now: The French Novel in
    the 21st Century.
  Oulipo: A Primer of Potential
    Literature.
GERALD MURNANE, *Barley Patch.*
  Inland.

YVES NAVARRE, *Our Share of Time.*
  Sweet Tooth.
DOROTHY NELSON, *In Night's City.*
  Tar and Feathers.
ESHKOL NEVO, *Homesick.*
WILFRIDO D. NOLLEDO, *But for the Lovers.*
FLANN O'BRIEN, *At Swim-Two-Birds.*
  At War.
  The Best of Myles.
  The Dalkey Archive.
  Further Cuttings.
  The Hard Life.
  The Poor Mouth.
  The Third Policeman.
CLAUDE OLLIER, *The Mise-en-Scène.*
  Wert and the Life Without End.
GIOVANNI ORELLI, *Walaschek's Dream.*
PATRIK OUŘEDNÍK, *Europeana.*
  The Opportune Moment, 1855.
BORIS PAHOR, *Necropolis.*
FERNANDO DEL PASO, *News from the Empire.*
  Palinuro of Mexico.
ROBERT PINGET, *The Inquisitory.*
  Mahu or The Material.
  Trio.
A. G. PORTA, *The No World Concerto.*
MANUEL PUIG, *Betrayed by Rita Hayworth.*
  The Buenos Aires Affair.
  Heartbreak Tango.
RAYMOND QUENEAU, *The Last Days.*
  Odile.
  Pierrot Mon Ami.
  Saint Glinglin.
ANN QUIN, *Berg.*
  Passages.
  Three.
  Tripticks.
ISHMAEL REED, *The Free-Lance Pallbearers.*
  The Last Days of Louisiana Red.
  Ishmael Reed: The Plays.
  Juice!
  Reckless Eyeballing.
  The Terrible Threes.
  The Terrible Twos.
  Yellow Back Radio Broke-Down.
JASIA REICHARDT, *15 Journeys from Warsaw*
    to London.
NOËLLE REVAZ, *With the Animals.*
JOÃO UBALDO RIBEIRO, *House of the*
    Fortunate Buddhas.
JEAN RICARDOU, *Place Names.*
RAINER MARIA RILKE, *The Notebooks of*
    Malte Laurids Brigge.
JULIÁN RÍOS, *The House of Ulysses.*
  Larva: A Midsummer Night's Babel.
  Poundemonium.
  Procession of Shadows.
AUGUSTO ROA BASTOS, *I the Supreme.*
DANIËL ROBBERECHTS, *Arriving in Avignon.*
JEAN ROLIN, *The Explosion of the*
    Radiator Hose.
OLIVIER ROLIN, *Hotel Crystal.*
ALIX CLEO ROUBAUD, *Alix's Journal.*
JACQUES ROUBAUD, *The Form of a*
    City Changes Faster, Alas, Than
    the Human Heart.
  The Great Fire of London.
  Hortense in Exile.
  Hortense Is Abducted.
  The Loop.
  Mathematics:
  The Plurality of Worlds of Lewis.

SELECTED DALKEY ARCHIVE TITLES

The Princess Hoppy.
Some Thing Black.
LEON S. ROUDIEZ, *French Fiction Revisited.*
RAYMOND ROUSSEL, *Impressions of Africa.*
VEDRANA RUDAN, *Night.*
STIG SÆTERBAKKEN, *Siamese.*
LYDIE SALVAYRE, *The Company of Ghosts.*
Everyday Life.
The Lecture.
Portrait of the Writer as a Domesticated Animal.
The Power of Flies.
LUIS RAFAEL SÁNCHEZ,
Macho Camacho's Beat.
SEVERO SARDUY, *Cobra & Maitreya.*
NATHALIE SARRAUTE,
Do You Hear Them?
Martereau.
The Planetarium.
ARNO SCHMIDT, *Collected Novellas.*
Collected Stories.
Nobodaddy's Children.
Two Novels.
ASAF SCHURR, *Motti.*
CHRISTINE SCHUTT, *Nightwork.*
GAIL SCOTT, *My Paris.*
DAMION SEARLS, *What We Were Doing and Where We Were Going.*
JUNE AKERS SEESE,
Is This What Other Women Feel Too?
What Waiting Really Means.
BERNARD SHARE, *Inish.*
Transit.
AURELIE SHEEHAN, *Jack Kerouac Is Pregnant.*
VIKTOR SHKLOVSKY, *Bowstring.*
Knight's Move.
A Sentimental Journey: Memoirs 1917–1922.
Energy of Delusion: A Book on Plot.
Literature and Cinematography.
Theory of Prose.
Third Factory.
Zoo, or Letters Not about Love.
CLAUDE SIMON, *The Invitation.*
PIERRE SINIAC, *The Collaborators.*
KJERSTI A. SKOMSVOLD, *The Faster I Walk, the Smaller I Am.*
JOSEF ŠKVORECKÝ, *The Engineer of Human Souls.*
GILBERT SORRENTINO,
Aberration of Starlight.
Blue Pastoral.
Crystal Vision.
Imaginative Qualities of Actual Things.
Mulligan Stew.
Pack of Lies.
Red the Fiend.
The Sky Changes.
Something Said.
Splendide-Hôtel.
Steelwork.
Under the Shadow.
W. M. SPACKMAN, *The Complete Fiction.*
ANDRZEJ STASIUK, *Dukla.*
Fado.
GERTRUDE STEIN, *Lucy Church Amiably.*
The Making of Americans.
A Novel of Thank You.
LARS SVENDSEN, *A Philosophy of Evil.*
PIOTR SZEWC, *Annihilation.*
GONÇALO M. TAVARES, *Jerusalem.*

Joseph Walser's Machine.
Learning to Pray in the Age of Technique.
LUCIAN DAN TEODOROVICI,
Our Circus Presents . . .
NIKANOR TERATOLOGEN, *Assisted Living.*
STEFAN THEMERSON, *Hobson's Island.*
The Mystery of the Sardine.
Tom Harris.
TAEKO TOMIOKA, *Building Waves.*
JOHN TOOMEY, *Sleepwalker.*
JEAN-PHILIPPE TOUSSAINT, *The Bathroom.*
Camera.
Monsieur.
Reticence.
Running Away.
Self-Portrait Abroad.
Television.
The Truth about Marie.
DUMITRU TSEPENEAG, *Hotel Europa.*
The Necessary Marriage.
Pigeon Post.
Vain Art of the Fugue.
ESTHER TUSQUETS, *Stranded.*
DUBRAVKA UGRESIC, *Lend Me Your Character.*
Thank You for Not Reading.
TOR ULVEN, *Replacement.*
MATI UNT, *Brecht at Night.*
Diary of a Blood Donor.
Things in the Night.
ÁLVARO URIBE AND OLIVIA SEARS, EDS.,
Best of Contemporary Mexican Fiction.
ELOY URROZ, *Friction.*
The Obstacles.
LUISA VALENZUELA, *Dark Desires and the Others.*
He Who Searches.
MARJA-LIISA VARTIO, *The Parson's Widow.*
PAUL VERHAEGHEN, *Omega Minor.*
AGLAJA VETERANYI, *Why the Child Is Cooking in the Polenta.*
BORIS VIAN, *Heartsnatcher.*
LLORENÇ VILLALONGA, *The Dolls' Room.*
TOOMAS VINT, *An Unending Landscape.*
ORNELA VORPSI, *The Country Where No One Ever Dies.*
AUSTRYN WAINHOUSE, *Hedyphagetica.*
PAUL WEST, *Words for a Deaf Daughter & Gala.*
CURTIS WHITE, *America's Magic Mountain.*
The Idea of Home.
Memories of My Father Watching TV.
Monstrous Possibility: An Invitation to Literary Politics.
Requiem.
DIANE WILLIAMS, *Excitability: Selected Stories.*
Romancer Erector.
DOUGLAS WOOLF, *Wall to Wall.*
Ya! & John-Juan.
JAY WRIGHT, *Polynomials and Pollen.*
The Presentable Art of Reading Absence.
PHILIP WYLIE, *Generation of Vipers.*
MARGUERITE YOUNG, *Angel in the Forest.*
Miss MacIntosh, My Darling.
REYOUNG, *Unbabbling.*
VLADO ŽABOT, *The Succubus.*
ZORAN ŽIVKOVIĆ, *Hidden Camera.*
LOUIS ZUKOFSKY, *Collected Fiction.*
VITOMIL ZUPAN, *Minuet for Guitar.*
SCOTT ZWIREN, *God Head.*